Francis Crawford Burkitt

The Old Latin and the Itala, with an appendix containing the

text of the S. Gallen palimpsest of Jeremiah

Francis Crawford Burkitt

The Old Latin and the Itala, with an appendix containing the text of the S. Gallen palimpsest of Jeremiah

ISBN/EAN: 9783337228910

Printed in Europe, USA, Canada, Australia, Japan

Cover: Foto ©Andreas Hilbeck / pixelio.de

More available books at **www.hansebooks.com**

CONTRIBUTIONS TO
BIBLICAL AND PATRISTIC LITERATURE

EDITED BY

J. ARMITAGE ROBINSON B.D.

HON. PH.D. GÖTTINGEN HON. D.D. HALLE
NORRISIAN PROFESSOR OF DIVINITY

VOL. IV.

No. 3. THE OLD LATIN AND THE ITALA

CAMBRIDGE
AT THE UNIVERSITY PRESS
1896

𝔏𝔬𝔫𝔡𝔬𝔫: C. J. CLAY AND SONS,
CAMBRIDGE UNIVERSITY PRESS WAREHOUSE,
AVE MARIA LANE.
𝔊𝔩𝔞𝔰𝔤𝔬𝔴: 263, ARGYLE STREET.

𝔏𝔢𝔦𝔭𝔷𝔦𝔤: F. A. BROCKHAUS.
𝔑𝔢𝔴 𝔜𝔬𝔯𝔨: MACMILLAN AND CO.

AND

THE ITALA

WITH AN APPENDIX CONTAINING

THE TEXT OF THE S. GALLEN PALIMPSEST

OF JEREMIAH

BY

F. C. BURKITT M.A.

CAMBRIDGE

AT THE UNIVERSITY PRESS

1896

Cambridge:

PRINTED BY J. AND C. F. CLAY,
AT THE UNIVERSITY PRESS.

TO THE REVEREND

WILLIAM SANDAY D.D.

THE LADY MARGARET'S PROFESSOR OF DIVINITY

IN THE UNIVERSITY OF OXFORD

IS DEDICATED

THIS ATTEMPT TO BUILD

BY THE METHODS HE HAS TAUGHT

ON THE FOUNDATIONS HE HAS LAID.

TABLE OF CONTENTS.

INTRODUCTION.

THE following Essays have grown out of a lecture delivered at Oxford during the Lent Term of the present year. My original object was not so much to give a general summary of what is known about Latin Versions of the Bible as to call attention to certain detached points of interest connected with the subject, which could be studied with more or less completeness by themselves. These points once settled, a firmer hold would be gained upon the general problems which confront the student in this complicated subject. One of these points, the identification of S. Augustine's *Itala* with the Vulgate, was of sufficient importance to expand into an Essay by itself. The rest of the lecture has been left as it was originally delivered, but I have added some Notes to what might appear the more hazardous statements in the text. These Notes will, I hope, serve to justify and to illustrate the positions I have been led to take, and to form an apology for the publication of the Essays.

To have come to novel conclusions after working at such familiar materials as the quotations of Tertullian and SS. Cyprian and Augustine fills me with some alarm for the correctness of my reasoning, and makes me wish to have the judgment of specialists upon my work. But whatever may be thought of the explanation of the Itala, here revived for the first time since the days of the compilation of the *Glossa Ordinaria*, I cannot but think that the story of Felix the Manichee, taken in connection with the undoubted use of the Vulgate in the *de Consensu Euangelistarum*, ought to modify current ideas of the composition of the New Testament in the African Church of the fifth century. In the present day S. Augustine is almost invariably considered as an

'Old Latin' authority for all parts of the Bible and in all his writings, and the cautions uttered by Sabatier himself (*Praef.* p. lvii) are generally unheeded.

The evidence for the use of the Septuagint version of Daniel in the early Latin Church does not seem to be so widely known as it should be. I have therefore given it somewhat fully. The early literary history of the book of Job in Latin is written here, I believe, for the first time.

The fragments of Jeremiah from S. Gallen are republished from the MS. Tischendorf's transcript is inaccurate and not very accessible, and the text of the MS is of sufficient interest to deserve a critical estimate of its value. The uncial types used on pp. 82—85 are those cut more than a hundred years ago for Kipling's edition of Codex Bezae. They must not of course be taken as accurately representing the shapes of the letters in the S. Gallen MS.

For convenience of reference I give a list of the chief Latin MSS of the N. Test. referred to in this volume, with their reputed dates.

a.   Cod. Vercellensis (iv), at Vercelli.
b.   „ Veronensis (v), at Verona.
c.   „ Colbertinus (xii), at Paris, from Languedoc.
d.   „ Bezae (vi), at Cambridge, from Southern Gaul (?).
e.   „ Palatinus (v), at Vienna, once at Trent.
f.   „ Brixianus (vi), at Brescia.
ff.   „ Corbeiensis 2 (vi), at Paris, from Corbie in Picardy.
h (evv.). Cod. Claromontanus (v—vii), at the Vatican. Only Mt in O. Latin.
h (apoc., act., cath. epp.). Cod. Floriacensis (vi—vii), at Paris, from Fleury on the Loire. A palimpsest, and very fragmentary.
i.   Cod. Vindobonensis (vii), at Vienna, once at Naples (Lc Mc).
k.   „ Bobiensis (v), at Turin, once at Bobbio (Mc Mt).
l.   „ Rehdigeranus (vii), at Breslau, once apparently at Verona. As this MS has a Vulgate base with occasional Old Latin readings it is called *reh* by Westcott and Hort.
m. Speculum [Ps-]Augustini. A collection of extracts from the Old and New Test., now edited in *Corp. Scr. Eccl. Lat.* vol. xii.

n. Cod. Sangallensis (v), at S. Gallen (fragments only). Two leaves, formerly called a_2, are now at Coire.

o. Cod. Sangallensis (vii), at S. Gallen. Last leaf of *n,* but in a later hand.

q. Cod. Monacensis (vii), at Munich, once at Freising.

r. „ Usserianus (? vii), at Dublin.

s. Fragmenta Ambrosiana (v—vi), at Milan (Lc).

t. Fragmenta Bernensia (vi), at Berne (Mc).

Among the best MSS of the Vulgate (following Wordsworth and White) are

A. Cod. Amiatinus.

C. „ Cavensis.

J. „ Foro-Juliensis.

M. „ Mediolanensis.

ℙ. „ Epternacensis.

A remark made by Dr Sanday at the head of his Essay on the text of *k* is so appropriate here that I will repeat it. He says: "In speaking of the 'texts' of *e, k,* Cyprian, &c. all the phenomena of those texts is meant. For our present purpose it is not necessary to discriminate between those of *reading,* which imply a difference in the underlying Greek, and those of *rendering,* where the variation is confined to the Latin. It is one of the immense advantages which the Latin possesses over the Greek text, that in any attempt to trace the genealogical relations of the different authorities, both these distinct classes of phenomena are available. In the Greek where there are no varieties of reading the text is necessarily colourless: in the Latin where this is the case differences of rendering may still afford clear indications of parentage; and it is by following out such indications that we are able to determine the mutual connexions and affinities of the MSS." (*Old-Latin Biblical Texts,* ii, p. xlii.)

THE OLD LATIN.

THE importance of the Latin Versions is not confined to their critical worth. Whatever value we may attach to the Latin interpretations of phrases occurring in the original Greek, it is undeniable that they have greatly influenced Western theological thought. Even the most literal version is also in some sense a commentary: the Latin indeed has none of the authority which sometimes attaches itself to the Syriac rendering of words and phrases originally spoken in an Aramaic dialect; yet to us it is historically more important. Many of our current conceptions of theological ideas have come to us through this Latin channel. The word 'eternal' is a familiar instance: another is Luther's famous difficulty with *agite paenitentiam* as an equivalent for μετανοεῖτε. But the influence in question is not confined to such serious matters. We more often think of the place of the Crucifixion as 'Calvary' than as 'Golgotha'. Again, from the history of the Latin Bible we learn, that Genesis, Exodus, Leviticus and Deuteronomy have always been called by their Greek names in Western Europe. In Tertullian we also find Arithmi instead of Numeri; yet as early as S. Cyprian the fourth book of the Pentateuch had a vernacular name, as it has among ourselves to-day.

Nevertheless the main worth of the Latin Versions to us is their critical value as 'authorities' for the text. Since the time of Lachmann the importance of the ancient codices of the Old Latin has always been recognised in New Testament criticism, even by scholars to whom 'Western' and 'corrupt' were in all cases synonymous terms. It is however to those who frankly accept Dr Hort's theory of the Syrian (or Antiochian) revision that this value is necessarily greatest, whatever may be their

feeling with regard to 'Western' texts. As long as in the
thousand Greek MSS of the Gospels were seen so many practically
independent authorities the evidence of a version might be
neglected. But Dr Hort's scheme so reduces the vast mass of
Greek witnesses, that the Western texts found in the early versions
regain much of their true *numerical* preponderance of attestation.
Moreover with a comparatively narrow basis of really weighty
Greek evidence, the possibility of sporadic error in our best MSS
must always be a factor in the account, and the value of a version
which in its origin at least was utterly independent of the eclectic
Greek texts of the fourth century becomes more evident than
ever.

I have spoken of the Old Latin *Version ;* the phrase is in itself
an assumption. *Tot exemplaria quot codices*—'every MS gives a
new type of text'—was the opinion of S. Jerome; and it is only
in quite recent years that criticism has got even a little beyond
this stage. At the same time the fact that our Latin authorities
often conspire together in variants found in hardly any extant
Greek MS was early noticed; whether there were one or two independent versions is a comparatively minor question in face of the
undoubted fact that the independent versions were few in number.
Among the more striking examples of the agreement of the Old
Latin codices (or of a majority of them) against most other
authorities are the substitution of Ps ii 7 'Thou art My Son, this
day have I begotten Thee' for the words uttered from heaven at
the Baptism in Lc iii 22; and the curious transposition of the
clauses of Lc ix 62, so that the verse runs 'No man that looketh
back and putteth his hand to the plough is fit for the kingdom of
God.' Neither of these is in any way supported by the Old
Syriac; so that they seem to be examples of readings geographi-
cally 'Western'.

In classifying our Old Latin authorities and attempting to
write a history of the texts they present, each group of the books
of the Bible must be treated separately. It is not till the seventh
century that we hear of Latin Pandects—great MSS of the whole
mass of Canonical Scriptures. A mere glance indeed at the extant
evidence for the various books shews the different ways in which
their text has been manipulated. The perplexing variety of the

Latin texts of the Gospels, the Psalms, and Isaiah, may be contrasted with the uninterrupted transmission of the book of Wisdom, a book highly esteemed and largely quoted, in which, strange to say, the text of S. Cyprian's citations hardly differs from the Clementine Vulgate. These however are extreme instances.

There are two books of the Old Testament which may be conveniently treated apart from the rest. The recensions in which they are extant are well known from Greek sources, and differ so extensively from one another as to be easily recognised in the corresponding Latin translations. These are the books of Daniel and Job.

The Old Latin authorities for the book of Daniel may be divided into two families, according as they follow the genuine LXX or the version of Theodotion. Theodotion's version is by far the most commonly met with. The purely Latin attestation for it begins with the 3rd cent. African tract *De Pascha computus* (dated AD 243) and Commodian[1]; it further includes Lucifer and the other 4th cent. writers[2]. But the ancient LXX version, as represented by the Cod. Chisianus and the Hexapla, is found in all the undoubtedly genuine works of Tertullian, including the Montanistic tracts written towards the end of his life. It is also found in the Commentary on the Apocalypse by S. Victorinus of Pettau, who was martyred in AD 303. The genuine chiliastic conclusion of this work, containing the clearest use of the LXX Daniel, was first published in the *Theologisches Literaturblatt* of April 26, 1895, by Dr Haussleiter of Greifswald; but the LXX text is to be traced in the earlier part of the work as well (*Migne* v 338, 340, and *Beatus*, pp. 440, 441). The quotations of S. Cyprian occupy a curious position midway between the LXX and Theodotion, suggesting that the change from the one version to the other was taking place in his own times, at least at Carthage[3].

Thus the earliest Latin version of Daniel as witnessed by

---

[1] See *Instruc* II 13 = Dan xiii 56 *Theod*; and *Apol* 267, 268 = Dan ix 24, 26 *Theod*.

[2] Theodotion's version is also found in the Latin translation of Irenaeus. It is therefore probable that S. Irenaeus himself used Theodotion, as the differences between the two Greek versions of Daniel are too great to have been altogether obscured in translation.

[3] See Note 1 at the end of this Essay.

Tertullian, by S. Victorinus of Pettau, and partly by S. Cyprian, was made from the LXX; a later Latin version was made from Theodotion. And so we see that we cannot write the history of the Latin versions from the evidence of MSS alone. For in the book of Daniel we have fragments of two magnificent Latin codices of the 5th cent., the *Weingarten* MS and the *Würzburg* Palimpsest; but both give Theodotion's version and shew no trace of the LXX text.

The language of all the Biblical quotations in *De Pascha computus* distinctly points to Africa, and its date is contemporary with S. Cyprian. Yet in the long quotation of Dan ix 25—27 it keeps to Theodotion throughout, agreeing indeed very closely with the first hand of B. This might suggest that we have evidence of early revision from the Greek even in the African Bible. The book of Daniel may however have been subjected to exceptional treatment; if Theodotion's version was to be preferred to the LXX, it was a question of the adoption of an entirely new work, not the gradual correction of one type of text by another. S. Cyprian's mixed text of Daniel never reappears except in those writers who directly quote the *Testimonia*, and it may never have existed as a Biblical text except in his own half-corrected MS. All other Latin authorities use a text wholly that of the LXX or wholly Theodotion's[1]. The fact that during the third century the African Church, following the example of the rest of Christendom, exchanged the LXX of this book for Theodotion need not make us reject the presumption that Greek MSS were less frequently met with in Africa than elsewhere, and that there, if anywhere, sporadic correction of the Latin version from Greek MSS of the Bible was uncommon.

But there is another consideration of more general interest connected with the substitution of Theodotion for the LXX in the book of Daniel. It is a remarkable fact that Ecclesiastical writers are quite silent about this important change. The utmost

---

[1] In 'Tert' *aduersus Iudaeos* the portions taken out of Tertullian *contra Marcion* iii follow the LXX; but in the earlier sections of *adv. Iudaeos* (e.g. § 8), to which there are no parallels in Tertullian, the quotations from Daniel follow Theodotion. Note that *concidentium* (*adv. Iudaeos* § 3), an interpolation in the text of Dan ii 35, appears to come directly from Cypr. *Test* ii 17.

that even the learned S. Jerome has to tell us upon the subject is
that the Church did not use the LXX in this book, but Theodotion: 'et hoc cur acciderit nescio' (Hieron. *Praef. in Daniel.*). No
more direct proof can be given that the silence of Ecclesiastical
writers is not a sufficient ground for assuming that revisions of
the Bible of which they tell us nothing were never made. I leave
it to my readers to apply this to the objections often urged against
the parallel cases of the Antiochian revision of the Greek text
of the New Testament, and of the transformation of the Old
Syriac into the present Syriac Vulgate.

The other case where the Old Latin authorities can at once be
divided by recensions is the book of Job. This book passed through
three stages in Greek. (1) In its original Greek form, as we know
from the express statements of Origen, about 400 lines (i.e. half-
verses of the Hebrew) were missing. Either they were absent
from the translator's MS, or, as is more probable, they were inten-
tionally omitted by him. This original state survives in the
Thebaic version published by Ciasca. (2) But such large *lacunae*
could not remain unnoticed after the publication of literal Greek
versions from the Hebrew, and at some period most, but not quite
all, of the missing lines were supplied from Theodotion. This is
the form found in most of the extant MSS, including אBAC.
(3) In the Hexapla Origen accurately filled up the gaps, placing
however all the lines borrowed from Theodotion under asterisks.
His work remains in several Greek MSS used by Field, and in the
Syro-Hexaplar version.

Now each of these three types of text is represented in the
pre-Vulgate Latin. S. Jerome translated Origen's revision into
Latin, reproducing the asterisks. His work survives in at least
two MSS, and it is the text printed by Sabatier. It was used
extensively by S. Augustine and the later African writers, but
they make no distinction between the passages marked with
asterisks and the rest ; all is quoted as of equal authority. Again,
the revision found in אBA etc. is represented in Latin by S.
Ambrose, who here as often exhibits a special type of text among
Latin authorities, due to direct dependence upon Greek sources.
But the original Latin version did not contain the interpolated
verses. This version is met with in the quotations of S. Cyprian

and Lucifer: in Spain it survived to the fifth century, as is shewn by the *Speculum* and Priscillian[1].

Only in these two books, Daniel and Job, can we treat the Latin versions in this summary fashion. In the other books the extant Greek recensions are for the most part so late and mixed that the Latin does not easily fit in with any. Take the case of the four books of Kings. Here we have two main types of Greek text. One of these is represented by B, and also by A when its loosely-fitting interpolations have been set aside; the other is the recension of Lucian. Now there is a good deal of evidence which connects the Old Latin with the 'Lucianic' text; but it would be a mistake to bring in the Old Latin as third century evidence for the Lucianic text as we know it, or indeed for the Lucianic *recension* properly so called. The Old Latin seems to me rather to represent one element, and that probably the most important, out of which the composite Lucianic text was constructed. Lucian's recension in fact corresponds in a way to the Antiochian text of the New Testament. Both are texts composed out of ancient elements welded together and polished down. A text akin to that underlying the Old Latin was a factor in each. In the case of the Gospels we actually possess in our numerous Greek, Latin and Syriac MSS continuous texts similar to the elements out of which the Antiochian text was constructed, and thus the Antiochian text rarely contains traces of an ancient text not better preserved elsewhere. But in the case of the books of Kings our Latin evidence is fragmentary, and there is no ancient Greek MS to take the place which Cod. Bezae occupies in the Gospels and Acts. Hence the importance of Lucian's recension, a mixed text with ancient elements otherwise unrepresented. If we had the Old Latin of the books of Kings in a complete and pure form the value of Lucian would be largely discounted. As it is, we can use Lucifer and the Vienna Palimpsest and the *Speculum* to prove the existence of ancient elements in Lucian: but we cannot use them as authenticating Lucian as a whole. I do not here refer to the margin of the *Codex Gothicus Legionensis* published by Vercellone, as it is by no means certain that this interesting

[1] For a justification of the statements in the text see Note II at the end of this Essay.

document does not represent readings extracted and translated from some Greek codex, so that it may have no connection with the Old Latin properly so called[1]. Moreover the literary history of the book of Daniel in Latin will warn us against trusting too implicitly to the evidence of Latin MSS unauthenticated by ancient quotations.

The Old Latin MSS of the Gospels.

The different fates which befel the earliest Latin versions of Daniel and Job,—the former disappearing at the end of the third century, the latter surviving, at least in Spain, till the fifth,—shew us how impossible it is to form an *a priori* judgment about the history of the most important section of the Bible, viz. the Four Gospels. Here the evidence is at once most abundant and most confusing.

A rough list of the Old Latin MSS of the Gospels is to be found in the Introduction to this essay. I need only remark here that we now possess at least fragments of sixteen codices that are unhesitatingly assigned to the 'Old Latin'. Of these only one, the Latin side of Codex Bezae, forms part of a bilingual MS. Four of the MSS are at least as old as Codex Bezae, while four more, *a*, *b*, *e* and *n*, are said to be yet older, dating in fact from a time when the Old Latin was in full Church use in many parts of Western Europe. These facts are worth bearing in mind, in view of the not unnatural tendency to overestimate the number and influence of bilingual codices in the Latin Church, or even to regard the history of the Latin versions as a sub-province of the criticism of Codex Bezae.

For the most part what we know about the *provenance* of our MSS tells us nothing which can help us to localise their text. The fact, for instance, that *n* (together with the Coire fragment of the same MS, commonly called a_2) was in all probability part of the original library of the great monastery of S. Gallen, does not give us any clue to the wanderings of the MS in the two centuries and a half which preceded the foundation of the Benedictine settlement there. Again, even if we accept the tradition that Cod.

---

[1] Compare for a parallel instance the Latin glosses in *Cod. rescript. Cryptoferratensis* (Γ') to Isaiah and Jeremiah.

Bobiensis (*k*) was once the private property of S. Columban, we are not helped towards the solution of the really important question,—where and why an African text, full of the strange clerical blunders which we find in the text of *k*, came to be transcribed in the generation before the Saint was born ?

In the case of the oldest MS (*a*), and of the youngest (*c*), a knowledge of the history of the MSS does however help us in the criticism of their contents. Cod. *a* (Vercellensis) is said to have been written at Vercelli, where it still remains, by the hand of S. Eusebius during his retreat from the Arians after the Council of Milan. S. Eusebius died before the Vulgate was begun, and is not known ever to have left N. Italy. Here then, if anywhere, we have a pre-Vulgate 'European' text. Its connection with S. Eusebius' friend Lucifer of Cagliari I shall touch upon at the end of this essay. Cod. *c* (Colbertinus), a MS of the 12th cent., came from Languedoc, the country of the Albigenses[1]. Only *among heretics* isolated from the rest of Western Christianity could an Old Latin text have been written at so late a period. In this case therefore our knowledge of the original home of the MS to a certain extent explains the character of its text.

The 'African' Text of the Gospels.

The first great step in the scientific classification of the Old Latin MSS of the Gospels was made in Dr Hort's letter to the *Academy* of Aug. 14, 1880, in which he for the first time pointed out the close connection of the texts of *k* (Bobiensis) and *e* (Palatinus) with the numerous and accurate quotations of S. Cyprian. Previously to this Codd. *a b c* and *i* had been assumed to represent the original and therefore presumably African form of the Latin Version, all variations from this arbitrary standard being put down to correction from Greek MSS.

Of these two codices *k* is more faithful to the Cyprianic text than *e*; but both are on quite a different plane from the rest of the Latin MSS. We may therefore take *k* and *e* to represent the

---

[1] Berger, *Histoire de la Vulgate*, pp. 74, 75. A curious parallel is furnished by a 13th cent. MS of the N.T., in which about half the text of the Acts is Old Latin of good quality. The MS originally came from Perpignan, and the Old Latin portion has lately been published by M. Berger (*Notices et Extraits*, XXXV, pt. i).

form in which the Gospels were read in Africa (or at least at
Carthage) as early as the middle of the third century. The only
other non-Patristic authorities which shew a distinctive 'African'
character are the contemporary corrections in the text of *n* (esp.
in Lc and Mc), which must have been made from a MS very like *e*;
and isolated sections of *c*, such as the last chapters of the Gospel
of S. Luke. The strongly African character of Lc xxiii, xxiv in
this MS is somewhat obscured by the fact that the well-known
Western Non-Interpolations in cap. xxiv—verses and clauses
omitted by *a b d e ff l r*—have been inserted into *c* from the
Vulgate, with the language of which they almost always verbally
agree, though the other verses of the context differ widely from it[1].

The character of this 'African' version differs much from other
Old Latin texts both in language and in the underlying Greek
text[2]. But one fact stands out above all others—its utter un-
likeness to the eclectic texts of the fourth century, both Greek and
Latin. For the most part the interpolations of this, the oldest
continuous Latin text of the Gospels which has come down to us,
are not the interpolations of the eclectic texts, and its omissions
are not their omissions: moreover its renderings are not the
renderings of the later revised Latin texts such as the Vulgate
and its immediate predecessors.

It is this note of singularity and independence which is the
chief characteristic of the 'African' version, whether in the Gospels
or elsewhere; not any positive quality of its own style considered
apart from other Latin versions of the Bible.

1.   Thus we find occasional transliterations of Greek words,
where other texts have vernacular renderings. Examples are

agape	1 Cor. xiii *passim* Cypr. *Test* III 3
anastasis	Mc xii 23 *k*
discolum	Mc x 24 *k*
martyria	Ps cxviii 2 Cypr. *Test* III 16
mons Eleon	Mc xiv 26 *k*, and Ac i 12 Aug. *contra Fel* i 4

In the titles of books we find not only *cata Mattheum, cata*

---

[1] See Note III at the end of this Essay.

[2] The only thorough investigation of any part of the African text is to be found
in Dr Sanday's Essay on *k* in *Old-Latin Biblical Texts*, vol. ii.

Lucan, etc., but in Cyprian also we have *in Paroemiis* (e.g. *Test* III 66), and *in Basilion* (i.e. Βασιλειῶν) for *in Regnorum* [*libro*].

2. Quite as often the opposite practice prevails. Several well known adaptations of Greek words either do not occur at all in the African texts or are found side by side with attempts at Latin equivalents. Examples are

similitudo	side by side with *parabola*
bene nuntiare	*euangelizare*
tinguere	*baptizare*

3. In the African texts many common words, familiar to us through the Vulgate or the service books, are represented by less usual synonyms. Among the more prominent examples are

illic	for *ibi*
nempe	*ergo*
si quo minus	*alioquin*
fuit (ἦν)	*erat*
claritas	*gloria*
sermo (λόγος)	*uerbum*
felix	*beatus*
discens	*discipulus*
pressura (most books)	*tribulatio* (Apoc)
colligere (exc. Ezech)	*congregare*
maledicere (ὀνειδίζειν)	*improperare*
saeculum (in S. Joh)	*mundus*

Among texts which thus assume an unfamiliar aspect in African documents a notable instance is Joh i 1, which appears in *Test* II 3 (codd. opt.) as *In principio fuit sermo*. In Joh viii 12 e and Cypr. *Ep* 63 have not *Lux Mundi* but *Lumen Saeculi*.

This unusual vocabulary is extremely useful to the critic: it shews the comparative independence of the African documents; it is also a most useful test for discovering whether documents of uncertain ancestry be 'African' or not,—'African', that is, in the sense in which the word has been so often used in this essay, viz. *homogeneous with the Biblical text used by S. Cyprian*.

For it can scarcely be maintained that differences of rendering such as these are dialectical in the ordinary sense of the word.

They can only in part be paralleled from the original works of African writers; it is absurd for instance to claim *sermo* or *saeculum* as a predominantly 'African' word, except in the sense that the translator of the Gospels (presumed from other considerations to have been an African by nationality) took these words as his rendering of the Johannine λόγος and the Johannine κόσμος, and mechanically retained them throughout. Indeed in so literal a version as the Old Latin there is not much room for dialectical peculiarities.

The most promising field for real 'Africanisms' would be, I should imagine, the common adverbial locutions and the smaller parts of speech generally[1]. Thus *illic* occurs in the African Fathers not only when they are giving the words of Scripture, but also in the formula of quotation *item illic*, where the Europeans use *item ibi*. In the Book of Rules composed by Tyconius, an African who flourished about 380 AD, *illic* occurs a dozen times, *ibi* never. Here then we seem to have a genuine Africanism.

But such clear instances are rare; and two passages from S. Augustine, in which he expressly declares the interchangeability of some of these synonyms, shew how little the difference of rendering corresponds to real difference of dialect. He says (*contra sermonem Arrianorum* 35): "*Glorificare* autem et *honorificare* et *clarificare* tria quidem uerba, sed una res est, quod Graece dicitur δοξάζειν; interpretum autem uarietate aliter atque aliter positum est in Latino." And again (*de Consensu Euangelistarum* iii 71): "Marcus [xvi 12] inquit...*Euntibus in uillam.* castellum quippe illud non absurde etiam *uillam* potuisse appellari ... et in codicibus quidem graecis magis agrum inuenimus quam uillam. agri autem nomine non *castella* tantum uerum etiam *municipia* et *coloniae* solent uocari extra ciuitatem, quae caput et quasi mater est ceterarum, unde metropolis appellatur." From the last sentence we may gather that though in S. Augustine's Africa the 'municipium' was larger than the 'castellum', either might quite well be used to indicate κώμη as an inhabited place inferior to the πόλις, which is constantly rendered by 'ciuitas'[2].

---

[1] See Note iv.
[2] See *O. Lat. Bibl. Texts*, ii 137 f.

The general criticism of the European documents has yet to be written. It is a task encompassed with peculiar difficulties. If the received theory of the Latin Versions be true—that they originated in Africa, and were adopted in Italy, Gaul and Spain with such changes as local usage seemed to recommend, and with occasional partial revisions from such Greek MSS as were available, —then we can indeed investigate the original African text, but the *original* European text is almost a contradiction in terms. The history of the European text would be that of a continuous development, or rather degeneration, from the African standard. This is however only a theory, though a very probable one; and it is held on the other hand by some scholars that there was an original European version independent of the African text. The question has a very practical issue. When one or two European authorities side with the Africans against the rest, are we to regard these 'African' readings as relics of a more ancient stage of the 'European' Latin when it was only half Europeanised? Or are these African readings mere excrescences in the true European text—like, for instance, the corrections in *n*?

The European MSS group themselves round the two great codices *a* (Vercellensis) and *b* (Veronensis); and of late there has been a disposition to look upon *b* as giving the truest picture of the European text. Mr White, whose acquaintance with the details of these MSS must be as great as any scholar's, says: "*b* seems to be almost a typical European MS, as the other MSS of European and of Italian origin, such as *a, f, h, i, q, r*, all resemble *b* more closely than they resemble each other."[1] He might indeed have added the Vulgate to this list of MSS. There is no doubt that *b* occupies a central position, and that its great rival *a* often has African renderings; the only question is whether *a* does not in this respect represent an altogether earlier stage of the European Latin than *b*. Nor is *a* entirely without followers. It is supported in Mt Mc Lc by the Swiss MS *n*, while in S. John (where the exemplar followed by *n* seems to have been corrected to the *b* text)

---

[1] *O. Lat. Bibl. Texts*, iii, p. xxxii.

the quotations of Lucifer of Cagliari generally agree with *a*. A still more important witness to the age of the text of *a* is Novatian of Rome (the contemporary of S. Cyprian), whose quotations are decidedly nearer to *a* than to *b*. And in this connection a remark in Dr Sanday's essay on *k* is well worthy of attention. Commenting on Mc xii 40 he says: "The older translators had great difficulty with προφάσει μακρὰ προσευχόμενοι, though they ended by hitting upon an admirable rendering in 'sub obtentu prolixae orationis' of *b*, adopted in Vulg."

This I believe to be what has often happened, though as a rule *b* is supported by *ff*, *f* and *q* as well as the Vulgate: in other words *b* is the oldest representative of that stage of the European text from which most of the later forms of the Old Latin, and finally the Vulgate, are descended[1].

Before taking leave of this part of the subject I should like to draw attention to a point of very great importance intimately connected with the history of the Latin versions. No feature in the textual criticism of the Gospels is more striking, or of more vital interest, than the Great Interpolations, such as Mt xvi 2, 3 (the Signs of the Sky), Mt xx 28 *fin.* ('Seek from little to increase'), Lc xxii 43, 44 (the Bloody Sweat), Joh v 3, 4 (the Descent of the Angel), and the story of the Woman taken in Adultery. Now the stronghold of these interpolations is the Old Latin. As we trace the history of the text of the N.T. in other languages we find the earliest form is free from these interpolations. In Greek they are absent from B and its allies; in Syriac they are absent from the Sinai Palimpsest, a MS with a very different text in other respects from B. But they seem to form an integral part of the earliest Latin version. They are especially characteristic of the African text: a fact all the more remarkable, as the best African documents often side with ℵB in rejecting the harmonistic and other ordinary additions found in most other authorities. The extant European documents often contain these great Interpolations, but in other cases they omit them, and as a rule they are supported in their choice by the 'Textus Receptus'. The European Latin thus seems to have been the channel by which some of these valuable fragments

---

[1] See Note IV on παραβολή.

of ancient tradition have found their way into the dominant
Ecclesiastical recensions of the fourth century. This by no means
inevitably implies that the passages in question were translated
from the Latin; it is equally consistent with the evidence to
suppose that the Antiochian revisers were sometimes guided in
their choice by the knowledge that this or that otherwise doubtful
passage was read by the Church of Rome or of Milan.

Quite distinct from these great additions to the true text is
a series of smaller interpolations, which cannot so certainly be
referred to independent sources, and seem rather to be due to the
inventiveness of scribes. From these the African text is comparatively free, while on the other hand the 'European' texts with
hardly an exception contain them all. It is difficult to separate
the study of both these classes of additions to the true text from
the well-known 'Western' additions to the Acts; these, it should
never be forgotten, are quite as characteristic of the African texts
of *h* (Floriacensis) and S. Cyprian as of Codex Bezae. The ultimate local source of all these interpolations is still quite obscure.
It is tempting to suppose that they may have originated at some
very early centre of Christianity such as Rome, and have been
thus early taken to Carthage, and preserved there through the
comparative isolation of Roman Africa from Greek influences[1].

But speculations of this kind do not take us beyond the region
of conjecture. I have only suggested them here for the benefit
of those who, like myself, believe that we shall not really advance
the study of these questions until the mutual relations of the
various forms of the European Latin have been placed on a
firmer basis by the laborious but scientific method of classifying
the peculiarities of the MSS and quotations which have come down
to us.

[1] See Note v.

NOTE I.

The use of the LXX text of Daniel in Latin writers.

That the Church used Theodotion's text of Daniel, and not the LXX, is a statement which has been commonly repeated since the days of S. Jerome. Nevertheless there remain considerable traces of the use of the LXX in the earlier stages of the Latin Church; a collection of the available evidence may therefore prove not uninteresting. Excluding S. Irenaeus as not truly a Latin Father, the four writers who quote Daniel sufficiently for our purpose are Tertullian, S. Cyprian, the author of *De Pascha Computus*, and S. Victorinus of Pettau. Of these the first and the last used the LXX, the author of *De Pascha Computus* used Theodotion, and S. Cyprian used a mixed text.

1. *Tertullian.*

Tertullian's quotations from Daniel are given below side by side with Origen's revision of the LXX as it stands in Dr Swete's edition. That edition here rests upon the Greek cursive *Cod. Chisianus* (87) and the Syro-Hexaplar version (Syr). Origen's work was provided with asterisks and obeli as in the other books of the Bible, the asterisk (*) being supposed to represent an addition from the Hebrew not found in the original LXX text, while the obelus (÷) marks words belonging indeed to the LXX but absent from the Hebrew. An interesting result of the present investigation is that we gain some idea of how much these marks are to be depended upon in our two authorities.

The quotations from 'Tert' *aduersus Iudaeos* are not included in this list.

Dan i 17

<table>
<tr><td>adv. Psych § 9 (Oehl. ɪ 863)</td><td>LXX</td></tr>
<tr><td>Dedit enim Deus adolescentulis</td><td>καὶ τοῖς νεανίσκοις ἔδωκεν ὁ κύριος</td></tr>
<tr><td>scientiam et intellegentiam</td><td>ἐπιστήμην καὶ σύνεσιν καὶ φρόνησιν</td></tr>
<tr><td>in omni litteratura</td><td>ἐν πάσῃ γραμματικῇ τέχνῃ</td></tr>
<tr><td>et Danieli</td><td>καὶ τῷ Δανιὴλ ἔδωκε σύνεσιν</td></tr>
<tr><td>in omni uerbo</td><td>ἐν παντὶ ῥήματι καὶ ὁράματι</td></tr>
<tr><td>et in somniis et in omni sophia.</td><td>καὶ ἐνυπνίοις καὶ ἐν πάσῃ σοφίᾳ.</td></tr>
</table>

÷ και εν π. σοφια 87

Theodotion has: καὶ τὰ παιδάρια ταῦτα, οἱ τέσσαρες αὐτοί, ἔδωκεν αὐτοῖς ὁ θεὸς σύνεσιν καὶ φρόνησιν ἐν πάσῃ γραμματικῇ καὶ σοφίᾳ· καὶ Δανιὴλ συνῆκεν ἐν πάσῃ ὁράσει καὶ ἐνυπνίοις. So B; A and Q have minor variations in the opening words.

Tertullian's words are not an exact quotation, but they contain the decisive phrase at the end corresponding to καὶ ἐν πάσῃ σοφίᾳ, a clause not found in Theodotion. The construction also of *Danieli* (= τῷ Δανιὴλ) agrees with LXX against Theodotion.

Dan ii 10—24

adv. Psych § 7 (Oehl. ɪ 862)

Circa somnium regis Babylonis omnes turbantur *sophistae*, negant ultro de praestantia humana posse cognosci, solus Daniel Deo fidens... spatium tridui postulat, *cum sua fraternitate ieiunat*, atque ita *orationibus* commendatis et ordinem et significationem somnii per omnia instruitur, tyranni *sophistis* parcitur, Deus glorificatur, Daniel honoratur.

The italicised portions of this summary occur only in the LXX. For the wise men of Babylon LXX has in *vv.* 14 and 24 σοφισταί, Theodotion σοφοί. In *vv.* 17[b], 18 LXX has τοῖς συνεταίροις ὑπέδειξε πάντα, [18]καὶ παρήγγειλε νηστείαν καὶ δέησιν καὶ τιμωρίαν, where Theodotion has τοῖς φίλοις αὐτοῦ ἐγνώρισεν τὸ ῥῆμα. [18]καὶ οἰκτειρμοὺς ἐζήτουν.

Dan ii 34, 44

adv. Marc iii § 7 (Oehl. ii 130)

et petra sane illa apud Danielem
de monte praecisa quae
imaginem saecularium regnorum
comminuet et conteret.

cf LXX

³⁴ἕως ὅτου ἐτμήθη λίθος ἐξ ὄρους...

⁴¹πατάξει δὲ καὶ ἀφανίσει τὰς
βασιλείας ταύτας...

Theodotion has in *ver.* 34 (+ οὗ A) ἀπεσχίσθη (ἐτμήθη AQ) λίθος ἐξ ὄρους, and in *ver.* 44 λεπτυνεῖ καὶ λικμήσει πάσας τὰς βασιλείας.

Here the text followed by Tertullian was nearer Theodotion. Compare however the quotation from Dan vii given below, which immediately follows this allusion.

Dan iii 16ᵇ—18

Scorp § 8 (Oehl. i 516)

Non habemus necessitatem
respondendi huic tuo imperio.

¹⁷est enim Deus noster

quem colimus
potens eruere nos
de fornace ignis

et ex manibus tuis.

¹⁸et tunc manifestum
fiet tibi
quod neque idolo tuo famulabimur,
nec imaginem tuam auream
quam statuisti
adorabimus.

LXX

οὐ χρείαν ἔχομεν ἡμεῖς
ἐπὶ τῇ ἐπιταγῇ ταύτῃ ἀποκριθῆναί
σοι.

¹⁷ἔστι γὰρ θεὸς
÷ ἐν οὐρανοῖς εἷς κύριος˟ ἡμῶν,
ὃν φοβούμεθα,
ὅς ἐστι δυνατὸς ἐξελέσθαι ἡμᾶς
ἐκ τῆς καμίνου τοῦ πυρὸς ✳ τῆς
καιομένης˟·
καὶ ἐκ τῶν χειρῶν σου, βασιλεῦ,
ἐξελεῖται ἡμᾶς·
¹⁸καὶ τότε φανερόν
σοι ἔσται, ✳ βασιλεῦ˟,
ὅτι οὔτε τῷ εἰδώλῳ σου λατρεύομεν
οὔτε τῇ εἰκόνι σου τῇ χρυσῇ,
ἣν ἔστησας,
[οὐ] προσκυνοῦμεν.

om ου Syr

Theodotion has according to cod B: Οὐ χρείαν ἔχομεν ἡμεῖς περὶ τοῦ ῥήματος τούτου ἀποκριθῆναί σοι. ¹⁷ἔστιν γὰρ θεός, ᾧ ἡμεῖς λατρεύομεν, δυνατὸς ἐξελέσθαι ἡμᾶς ἐκ τῆς καμίνου τοῦ πυρὸς τῆς καιομένης· καὶ ἐκ τῶν χειρῶν σου, βασιλεῦ, ῥύσεται ἡμᾶς· καὶ ἐὰν μή, γνωστὸν ἔστω σοι, βασιλεῦ, ὅτι τοῖς θεοῖς σου οὐ λατρεύομεν καὶ τῇ εἰκόνι ᾗ ἔστησας οὐ προσκυνοῦμεν.

The following are the more important variants of AQ.   17 θεος] + ημων εν ουρανοις Bᵃᵇ ᵐᵍ, ο θ͞ς ημων εν ουνοις A   18 εστω] εσται Q   εικονι] + τη χρυση AQ

Here the spaced type exhibits seven points where Theodotion differs from the united evidence of LXX and Tertullian.

In *de Res. Carn* § 58 (Oehl. II 545) and *de Orat* § 15 (Oehl. I 567) the *sarabarae* and *tiarae* of Shadrach and his companions are mentioned. Both garments occur in the LXX, τὰς τιάρας Dan iii 21 where they are thrown into the flames, and τὰ σαράβαρα Dan iii 94 where they come out. In Dan iii 21, according to Theodotion, both garments are mentioned together.

Dan iii 92 (25)

adv. Marc iv § 10 (Oehl. II 179)

...nomen sortitus est Christi, et appellationem *filii hominis*, Iesus scilicet Creatoris. hic erat uisus Babylonis regi in *fornace* cum martyribus suis *quartus, tamquam filius hominis*.

adv. Marc iv § 21 (Oehl. II 213)

Perspice...cum rege Babylonio *fornacem* eius *ardentem*, et inuenies illic *tamquam filium hominis*; nondum enim uere erat, nondum scilicet natus ex homine.

adv. Prax § 16 (Oehl. II 676)

in *fornace* Babylonii regis *quartus* apparuit, quamquam *filius hominis* est dictus.

LXX : καὶ ἡ ὅρασις τοῦ τετάρτου ὁμοίωμα ἀγγέλου θεοῦ.

Theodotion : καὶ ἡ ὅρασις τοῦ τετάρτου ὁμοία υἱῷ θεοῦ.

The original Aramaic is רמה לבר אלהין. There is, I believe, no authority which supports Tertullian here.

In *de Paenit* § 12 (Oehl. II 664) and *de Pat* § 13 (Oehl. II 610) Tertullian uses the phrase 'septenni squalore'. This is nearer the ἔτη ἑπτά of LXX in Dan iv 29 than the ἑπτὰ καιροὶ of Theodotion.

Dan vii 10

adv. Prax § 3 (Oehl. ıı 657)	LXX
Milies centies centena milia	χίλιαι χιλιάδες
adsistebant ei	ἐθεράπευον αὐτὸν
et milies centena milia	καὶ μύριαι μυριάδες
apparebant ei.	παρειστήκεισαν αὐτῷ.

approperabant ei *codd.*

Theodotion has χίλιαι χιλιάδες ἐλειτούργουν αὐτῷ, καὶ μύριαι μυριάδες παρ[ε]ιστήκεισαν αὐτῷ, which is also found in Justin *Tryph* § 31. The inversion of the clauses witnessed by Tertullian is found in S. Clement of Rome (*Ep* § 34), but with ἐλειτούργουν αὐτῷ instead of ἐθεράπευον αὐτόν[1].

Dan vii 13, 14

adv. Marc iii § 7 (Oehl. ıı 130)	LXX
Et ecce cum nubibus caeli	καὶ ἰδοὺ ἐπὶ τῶν νεφελῶν τοῦ οὐρανοῦ
tamquam filius hominis ueniens,	ὡς υἱὸς ἀνθρώπου ἤρχετο,
uenit usque ad ueterum dierum,	καὶ ὡς παλαιὸς ἡμερῶν
[et] aderat in conspectu eius,	παρῆν·
et qui adsistebant adduxerunt illum.	καὶ οἱ παρεστηκότες παρῆσαν αὐτῷ.
¹⁴et data est ei potestas regia	¹⁴καὶ ἐδόθη αὐτῷ ἐξουσία * καὶ τιμὴ βασιλική˟,
et omnes nationes terrae	καὶ πάντα τὰ ἔθνη τῆς γῆς
secundum genera	κατὰ γένη
et omnis gloria famulabunda,	καὶ πᾶσα δόξα αὐτῷ λατρεύουσα·
et potestas eius usque in aeuum	καὶ ἡ ἐξουσία αὐτοῦ ἐξουσία αἰώνιος
quae non auferetur,	ἥτις οὐ μὴ ἀρθῇ,
et regnum eius	καὶ ἡ βασιλεία αὐτοῦ,
quod non uitiabitur.	ἥτις οὐ μὴ φθαρῇ.

---

[1] *Apparebant* (=ἐθεράπευον apparently) also occurs in Tyconius (*Reg* p. 60), but the clauses are not inverted. In Tyc 2, in an allusion to Dan ii 34, 45, *commotuisse* appears to correspond rather to the συνηλόησε of LXX than to the ἐλέπτυνεν of Theodotion. On the other hand the very curious reference in Tyc 5 to Dan xi 36, 38 is nearer Theodotion.

Variants of Tertullian

adv. Marc iv § 39 (Oehl. II 264)

Ecce cum caeli nubibus tamquam filius hominis adueniens, *et cetera.* Et data est illi regia potestas...et gloria omnis scruiens illi, et potestas eius aeterna quae non auferetur, et regnum eius quod non corrumpetur.

Variants of Justin *Tryph* § 31

ἐπὶ] μετὰ ·

ἤρχετο...παρῆν] ἐρχόμενος· καὶ ἦλθεν ἕως τοῦ παλαιοῦ τῶν ἡμερῶν καὶ παρῆν ἐνώπιον αὐτοῦ

παρῆσαν αὐτῷ] προσήγαγον αὐτόν

αὐτῷ λατρεύουσα] om. αὐτῷ

ἥτις 2°] om. (= Cypr 92)

Compare also

de Carne Christ § 15 et Daniel: et super nubes tamquam filius hominis.

adv. Marc iii § 24: illo scilicet filio hominis ueniente in nubibus secundum Danielem.

adv. Marc iv § 10: filius hominis ueniens cum caeli nubibus.

Theodotion has: καὶ ἰδοὺ μετὰ (ἐπὶ Q) τῶν νεφελῶν τοῦ οὐρανοῦ ὡς υἱὸς ἀνθρώπου ἐρχόμενος, καὶ ἕως τοῦ παλαιοῦ τῶν ἡμερῶν ἔφθασεν· καὶ π ρ ο σ ή χ θ η αὐτῷ. ¹⁴καὶ αὐτῷ ἐδόθη ἡ ἀρχὴ καὶ ἡ τ ι μ ὴ καὶ ἡ βασιλεία, καὶ πάντες οἱ λαοί, φυλαί, καὶ γλῶσσαι δουλεύουσιν αὐτῷ· ἡ ἐξουσία αὐτοῦ ἐξουσία αἰώνιος ἥτις οὐ παρελεύσεται, καὶ ἡ βασιλεία αὐτοῦ οὐ διαφθαρήσεται.

I have marked the peculiarities of Theodotion which are represented neither in Tertullian nor LXX by spaced type. What however is most important to observe here is the close agreement of Tertullian with Justin Martyr. The Greek text implied by Tertullian does not differ from that of our only MS of Justin except in three small points. In *ver.* 13 the MS of Justin inserts καί between ἐρχόμενος and ἦλθεν, and in *ver.* 14 it has the full phrase ἐξουσία καὶ τιμὴ βασιλική. In these two points Tertullian is supported by Cypr 92 (see below), and a glance at the Hexaplar text shews that in the second at least Tertullian preserves the true reading. In the Hexaplar MSS the *metobelus* marking the end of an interpolation has been placed after βασιλική instead of after τιμή, so that the words καὶ τιμή are probably an interpolation in Justin. On the other hand Cyprian and Justin both omit the second ἥτις.

The remainder of Tertullian's references to Daniel consist of allusions to Dan ix, x, in *adv. Psychicos*, which where they follow the Biblical text agree with LXX against Theodotion.

Dan ix 1—4, 21, 23

adv. Psych § 7 (Oehl. I 862)

¹ᵃanno primo regis Darii

LXX

¹Ἔτους πρώτου ἐπὶ Δαρείου τοῦ Ξέρξου...

²ᵇ*cum ex recogitatu*

praedicatorum temporum

ab Hieremia
³dedit faciem suam Deo

in ieiuniis et sacco et cinere

²ᵇἐγὼ Δανιὴλ διενοήθην ἐν ταῖς βίβλοις

τὸν ἀριθμὸν τῶν ἐτῶν ὅτε ἐγένετο πρόσταγμα τῇ γῇ

ἐπὶ Ἱερεμίαν τὸν προφήτην...
³καὶ ἔδωκα τὸ πρόσωπόν μου ἐπὶ Κύριον τὸν θεὸν

εὑρεῖν προσευχὴν καὶ ἔλεος
ἐν νηστείαις καὶ σάκκῳ καὶ σποδῷ.

adv. Psych § 10 (Oehl. 1 867)
³...Daniel, anno primo regis Darii
cum ieiunus in sacco et cinere

⁴καὶ προσηυξάμην πρὸς Κύριον τὸν θεόν·

⁴exomologesin Deo ageret,
²¹Et adhuc *inquit*
loquente me in oratione,
ecce uir quem uideram
in somnis initio
uelociter uolans
appropinquauit mihi
quasi hora uespertini sacrificii.

ἐξωμολογησάμην...
²¹καὶ ἔτι
λαλοῦντός μου ἐν τῇ προσευχῇ μου,
καὶ ἰδοὺ ὁ ἀνὴρ ὃν εἶδον
ἐν τῷ ὕπνῳ μου τὴν ἀρχήν,
Γαβριήλ, τάχει φερόμενος
προσήγγισέ μοι
ἐν ὥρᾳ θυσίας ἑσπερινῆς.

adv. Psych § 7 (Oehl. 1 862)
²¹ᵇ*ueni inquit* demonstrare tibi
qua tenus miserabilis es.

²¹ᵇ...καὶ ἐγὼ ἦλθον ὑποδεῖξαί σοι ὅτι ἐλεεινὸς εἶ.

3 in ieiuniis] *om.* in *Ed. princ.*

cum ieiunus] cum ieiuniis *Ed. princ.*

Dan x 1—12

adv. Psych § 9 (Oehl. 1 863)
¹Anno *denique* tertio
Cyri regis Persarum
cum in recogitatu
incidisset uisionis...

LXX
¹Ἐν τῷ ἐνιαυτῷ τῷ πρώτῳ
Κύρου τοῦ βασιλέως Περσῶν...
...διενοήθην...ἐν ὁράματι

1 in recogitatu] regicogitatum *Ed. princ.*

1 Theod has τρίτῳ for πρώτῳ with Tert, but differs from both LXX and Tert in having ἄλιμμα for ἔλαιον, ἀνὴρ ἐπιθυμιῶν for ἄνθρωπος ἐλεεινὸς εἶ, κακωθῆναι for ταπεινωθῆναι, and in other points.

[2]In illis *inquit* diebus	[2]ἐν ταῖς ἡμέραις
ego Daniel eram lugens	ἐγὼ Δανιὴλ ἤμην πενθῶν
per tres hebdomadas,	τρεῖς ἑβδομάδας
[3]panem suauem non edi,	[3]ἄρτον ἐπιθυμιῶν οὐκ ἔφαγον
caro et uinum	καὶ κρέας καὶ οἶνος
non introierunt in os meum,	οὐκ εἰσῆλθεν εἰς τὸ στόμα μου
oleo unctus non sum,	ἔλαιον οὐκ ἠλειψάμην
donec consummarentur	ἕως τοῦ συντελέσαι με
tres hebdomades,	τὰς τρεῖς ἑβδομάδας τῶν ἡμερῶν.
quibus transactis angelus	
emissus est taliter alloquens:	[11]καὶ εἶπε μοι
[11a]Daniel homo es miserabilis,	Δανιήλ, ἄνθρωπος ἐλεεινὸς εἶ·...
[12b]ne timueris,	[12b]Μὴ φοβοῦ, Δανιήλ.
quoniam ex die prima	ὅτι ἀπὸ τῆς ἡμέρας τῆς πρώτης
qua dedisti animam tuam	ἧς ἔδωκας τὸ πρόσωπόν σου
recogitatui et humiliationi	διανοηθῆναι καὶ ταπεινωθῆναι
coram Deo	ἐναντίον κυρίου τοῦ θεοῦ σου,
exauditum est uerbum tuum,	εἰσηκούσθη τὸ ῥῆμά σου,
et ego introiui uerbo tuo.	καὶ ἐγὼ εἰσῆλθον τῷ ῥήματί σου.

2 lugens] legens *Ed. princ.*

The general result of this lengthy comparison may be stated in a few words. The text of Daniel used by Tertullian is a form of the LXX differing slightly from Origen's edition, but agreeing most closely with the quotations of Justin Martyr[1].

2. S. Cyprian.

The use of the LXX of Daniel once recognised in the Latin Church from a study of the quotations of Tertullian, it will not be necessary to treat S. Cyprian in such detail. I give below his not very numerous quotations from Daniel, marking what is distinc-

[1] I cannot resist adding two very important deductions, which immediately follow from what has been stated above, though they deal with questions not directly connected with the Old Latin. The first is, that the small range of pre-Hexaplaric variants in the LXX text of Daniel now known to us comes from the poverty of our material rather than from the good preservation of the text. The second deduction is, that the text of Justin's quotations is very fairly preserved. Justin's text rests upon a single late MS, and it has been conjectured (e.g. by Hatch, *Essays in Biblical Greek*, p. 190) that the longer quotations are entirely untrustworthy. But the almost complete agreement of Justin's long quotation of Dan vii 9—28 in *Tryph* § 31 with the text of Tertullian, wherever the two quotations run parallel, shews that no systematic alterations of this kind have been made.

tively from the LXX in **bold-face** type, and what is distinctively from Theodotion in *italics*. In quoting the *Testimonia* I have chiefly followed Hartel's L and the Oxford MS O_1 (*O. Lat. Bibl. Texts*, ii 123).

Test ii 17 (Hartel 84) = Dan ii 31—35

Et ecce imago **nimis** magna, et contemplatio eius imaginis metuenda et elata sta**bat contra** te, [32]*cuius* caput **fuit ex** auro bono, pectus et brachia *eius* argentea, uenter et femora aerea, [33]pedes autem ex parte **quidem** ferrei ex parte **autem** fictiles; [34]quoad usque abscisus est lapis de monte sine manibus concidentium, et percussit imaginem super pedes ferreos [et] fictiles et *comminuit* eos [35]**minut**atim. et **factum** est **simul** ferrum **et** testa **et** aeramentum **et** argentum **et** aurum— facta sunt **minuta** quasi **palea** aut *puluis* **in** area *aestate*, et **uentilauit illa uentus ita ut nihil remanserit ex illis,** et lapis qui percussit imaginem factus est mons magnus et inpleuit totam terram.

Selected variants (*incl.* Firmicus Maternus 20).   31 imago, imago *Firm* ipsius *Firm*   33 quidem] *om.* O_1 34 abscissus LMB   ferreos et] *om.* A; *om.* et BO_1*   35 aut] ut *Firm*   remanserint LO_1*   ex] in A *Firm*; *om.* BO_1O_3

Test iii 10 (Hart. 121); *ad Fort* 11 (Hart. 337); *Ep* 6 (Hart. 483); *Ep* 58 (Hart. 660)   Dan iii 16—18

[16]Responderunt **autem** Sidrac Misac Abdenago, **et** dix**erunt** *regi*: Nabuchodonosor rex, non opus est nobis de hoc *uerbo* respondere tibi. [17]est enim Deus cui *nos seruimus* potens eripere nos de camino ignis *ardentis*; et de manibus tuis, rex, *liberabit* nos. [18]et *si non, notum sit* tibi quia *diis* tuis non seruimus et imaginem auream quam statuisti non adoramus.

16 resp....dix.] *om.* ad Fort, Epp   uerbo] sermone M(*Test*) Q(*Ep* 6) 17 rex] *om.* Ep 58 M(*Test*) Q(*Ep* 6)   18 si non] *om.* W (*Test*)   quoniam *Ep* 6 A (*Test*)   deseruimus LBO$_1$ (*Test*)

de Laps 31 (Hartel 260) = Dan iii 25

Stans Azarias precatus est et aperuit os suum **et exomologesim faciebat Deo simul cum sodalibus suis** in medio igni.

de Dom. Or 8 (Hartel 271) = Dan iii 51

Tunc illi tres quasi ex uno ore hymnum canebant et benedicebant [Deum].

quasi] tanquam S   deum] S; dnm G; *om.* W

de Op. et Eleemos 5 (Hartel 377) = Dan iv 24

Propterea, rex, consilium meum placeat tibi, et peccata tua eleemosynis redime, *et iniustitias tuas miserationibus pauperum,* et *erit Deus patiens peccatis tuis.*

Test ii 26 (Hartel 92) = Dan vii 13, 14 (cf. Tert quoted above, p. 22 f.)

Videbam in uisu nocte, et ecce **in** nubibus caeli quasi filius hominis ueniens; **uenit** usque ad ueterum dierum et stetit in conspectu eius, et **qui adsistebant obtulerunt** cum. [14]et data est ei **potestas regia,** et omnes reges **terrae per genus, et omnis claritas** ser**uiens** ei, et potestas eius aeterna quae non auferetur et regnum eius non corrumpetur.

nocte] noctes L*; noctis B   per genus] et regnum *Firmicus Maternus*
seruient B *Firm*

de Laps 31 (Hartel 260) = Dan ix 4—6

(Daniel quoque...in sacco ac cinere uolutatur exomologesim faciens dolenter et dicens:) Domine Deus magnus et **fortis et metuendus** qui seruas testamentum et miserationem eis qui te diligunt et conseruant **inperia** tua. [5]peccauimus, facinus admisimus, **inpii fuimus,** transgressi sumus ac **deseruimus** praecepta tua et iudicia tua; [6]non audiuimus **puerorum** tuorum prophetarum qu**ae** locuti sunt in nomine tuo **super** reges nostros et omnes gentes et **super** omnem terram. tibi Domine, tibi iustitia; nobis autem confusio.

Test i 4 (Hartel 42) = Dan xii 4[b], 7[b]

Muni sermones et signa librum usque ad tempus consummationis, quoad *discant* multi et inpleatur *agnitio.* [7b]quoniam *cum* fiet dispersio *cognoscent* omnia haec.

ad Fort 11 (Hartel 337); *Ep* 58 (Hartel 661) = Dan xiv 5

Nihil colo **ego nisi Dominum** Deum meum qui condidit caelum et terram.

The difference of types makes clearly evident the mixed character of the text in these nineteen verses. Dan iv 24 and xii 4, 7 are wholly from Theodotion. On the other hand the quotations from the additions to the original Daniel—two verses from the

Song of the Three Children and one from Bel and the Dragon—
predominantly follow the LXX.

Turning to the verses which run parallel with the quotations
of Tertullian, it will be noticed at once that where S. Cyprian uses
the LXX his text is in fundamental agreement with them, in spite
of some difference in Latinity. They both in fact here use the
peculiar form of the LXX found in Justin Martyr. Nevertheless
S. Cyprian does not use altogether the same text as Tertullian.
It might have been conjectured that both Fathers quoted from the
same mixed version of LXX and Theodotion, and that Tertullian
had happened to quote only passages where the LXX element
largely predominates, while on the other hand the element from
Theodotion is clearly visible in S. Cyprian. But this cannot be
the case. Dan iii 16—18 is cited by both writers, in Tertullian
from the LXX, but in S. Cyprian almost entirely from Theodotion.

It is not necessary to conjecture a fresh translation into Latin
of a corrupted LXX text to account for the peculiarities of S.
Cyprian's Daniel. We know from *de Paschu Computus* that a
pure version from Theodotion was current in Africa in the life-
time of S. Cyprian. We also see from a comparison of S. Cyprian's
quotations with those of Tertullian that where he follows the LXX
he agrees with Tertullian, i.e. with the primitive African version.
It is therefore probable that his MS was a copy of the old Latin
version from the LXX, half-corrected to the new Latin version
from Theodotion. Traces of the process can yet be seen. In Dan
ii 35 כְּעוּר 'like chaff' is translated by LXX ὡσεὶ λεπτότερον
ἀχύρου, but by Theodotion ὡσεὶ κονιορτός. S. Cyprian has
minuta quasi palea aut puluis. The last two words are evidently
a marginal gloss from Theodotion, which has been *added* to S.
Cyprian's form of the LXX reading. That S. Cyprian's text of
Daniel reappears in Firmicus Maternus, and partly in Lactantius,
causes no difficulty; here, as elsewhere, these writers copy the
Biblical passages directly from the *Testimonia.*

Corruption from Theodotion does not however explain all the
peculiarities of S. Cyprian's citations. In many points his text in
passages which predominantly follow the LXX differs both from it
and from Theodotion. This feature, remarkable in so accurate a
quoter as S. Cyprian, must be taken in conjunction with his agree-

ment with Justin and Tertullian in vii 13, 14. It is evident that the Origenian recension was not the only form in which the LXX text of Daniel was circulated in early times[1].

3. S. Victorinus of Pettau.

The only non-African Latin evidence for the LXX Daniel is found in the scholia of S. Victorinus of Pettau upon the Apocalypse. The clearest allusions to Daniel occur in the lately recovered conclusion to the work, published for the first time in the *Theologisches Literaturblatt* of Apr. 26, 1895 by Prof. Haussleiter from MS Ottob. 3288 in the Vatican (= A). This MS is late (15th cent.) and very corrupt; I give therefore an emended text with the various readings of the MS, and of Dr Haussleiter's text, in the notes. As in the case of S. Cyprian, readings agreeing with the LXX against Theodotion are marked in **bold-face** type. The extract begins at *Th. Ltbt.* col 197, line 23.

Dan ii 40 Quartum autem regnum durissimum et potentissimum tamquam ferrum, quod domat omnia et omnem **arborem**
41, 43 **excidet.** Et in nouissimo **in se,** inquit, tamquam testa ferrum mixtum miscebuntur homines, et **non erunt con-**
44ᵃ **cordes neque consentanei.** Et in illis **temporibus**
vii 18 suscitabit Dominus Deus regnum **aliud,** quod suscipient
ii 44ᵇ inquit, sancti Summi Domini regnum, et regnum hoc alia gens non indagabit, namque Dominus percutiet et indagabit omnia regna terrae, et ipsud manebit in perpetuum.

potissimum A   omnia] *Haussl*; oram A   arborem] ualorem A *Haussl*
iu se] ipse A; *om. Haussl*   testa] testum A (*cf.* Iren v 26); testae *Haussl*   in
illis] *Haussl*; michi A   regnum] A; regum *Haussl*   omnia regna terrae]
uiam regnature A; uniuersa regna *Haussl*

---

[1] A full discussion of the composition of 'Tert' *adv. Iudaeos* ought to follow here, but I am unwilling to write an Excursus to an Excursus, and shall confine myself to stating the main facts concerning the text of Daniel found in the work. (1) In the sections borrowed from Tert *adv. Marc* iii, the *adv. Iudaeos* mainly follows the text of Tert. Where it differs, it almost invariably agrees with the *Testimonia.* (2) In the sections not taken from *adv. Marc* there are many points of contact with the *Testimonia.* One very striking instance, the addition of *concidentium* to Dan ii 34, is noticed in the text of this Essay, p. 7, note. (3) Dan ix 24—27, a passage not quoted by S. Cyprian, is quoted in *adv. Iudaeos* § 9 from Theodotion. The same verses are quoted in *de Pascha Computus,* and the two

I expect that in the MS 'oram' is written o͞i͞a, 'ipse' is written i͞s͞e, and 'uiam regnature' u͞i͞a regna t͞r͞e.

The corresponding passages in the LXX Greek are

ver. 40 καὶ βασιλεία τετάρτη ἰσχυρὰ * ὡς ὁ σίδηρος˟ ὥσπερ ὁ σίδηρος ὁ δαμάζων πάντα, καὶ * ὡς ὁ σίδηρος˟ πᾶν δένδρον ἐκκόπτων·...

When the interpolations under asterisks are removed, this agrees verbally with S. Victorinus, as restored. Theodotion is quite different, and has nothing about cutting down trees.

ver. 41, 43 καὶ...βασιλεία ἄλλη διμερὴς ἔσται ἐν αὐτῇ... 43καὶ ὡς εἶδες τὸν σίδηρον ἀναμεμιγμένον ἅμα τῷ πηλίνῳ ὀστράκῳ, καὶ συμμιγεῖς ἔσονται εἰς γένεσιν ἀνθρώπων. οὐκ ἔσονται δὲ ὁμονοοῦντες οὔτε εὐνοοῦντες ἀλλήλοις...

Here again the agreement of S. Victorinus with LXX is very marked. Theodotion's version of the last clause quoted is καὶ οὐκ ἔσονται προσκολλώμενοι οὗτος μετὰ τούτου.

The LXX version of the remaining clauses alluded to is

ver. 44ᵃ καὶ ἐν τοῖς χρόνοις τῶν βασιλέων τούτων στήσει ὁ θεὸς τοῦ οὐρανοῦ βασιλείαν ἄλλην.

ver. 44ᵇ καὶ αὕτη ἡ βασιλεία ἄλλο ἔθνος οὐ μὴ ἐάσῃ, πατάξει δὲ καὶ ἀφανίσει τὰς βασιλείας ταύτας.

Dan vii 18 both in LXX and Theod is παραλήψονται τὴν βασιλείαν ἅγιοι Ὑψίστου.

Immediately preceding the extracts here given, the last clause of Dan ii 35 is referred to with a text which evidently implies ἐπλήρωσεν as in Theodotion and Cypr. *Test* II 17, not ἐπάταξε as in the Hexaplar LXX.

Besides these clear instances of the use of the LXX of Daniel there are two allusions to Dan xi 37, 38, 45 in S. Victorinus (*Migne*, v 338, 340 = Beatus, p. 441, 440). For the sake of completeness I give them below with the corresponding LXX.

quotations, though differing in Latinity, agree in supporting B*, though the gloss in ix 27 is also known to the author of *adv. Iudaeos*. It would indeed be remarkable, if the disputed treatise *adv. Iudaeos* were really the work of Tertullian, that the only use of Theodotion in all his works should occur there, and that the quotations in it should have such a tendency to agree with the *Testimonia*.

Beatus, p. 441. *Desideria mulierum non cognoscet.*

cf. Dan xi 37 ἐν ἐπιθυμίᾳ γυναικὸς οὐ μὴ προνοηθῇ.

Beatus, p. 441. *Et nullum Deum patrum suorum cognoscet.*

cf. Dan xi 38 καὶ θεὸν ὃν οὐκ ἔγνωσαν οἱ πατέρες αὐτοῦ τιμήσει.

Beatus, p. 440. *Statuit templum suum inter maria super montem inclytum et sanctum.*

cf. Dan xi 45 καὶ στήσει αὐτοῦ τὴν σκηνὴν τότε ἀνὰ μέσον τῶν θαλασσῶν καὶ τοῦ ὄρους τῆς θελήσεως τοῦ ἁγίου.

If the resemblance between these curious allusions and the LXX text is but small, they resemble the text of Theodotion even less. It is the quotation of ii 43 cited above which makes a decisive case for the use of the LXX text of Daniel by S. Victorinus; but it was necessary to give his other allusions to the book, lest it should be thought that he used Theodotion elsewhere.

The text of Job in Latin Fathers.

1. S. Cyprian quotes in all only sixteen verses from the book
of Job, but it is clear from *Test* III 1 that his text omitted the first
half of xxix 13, which is one of the στίχοι derived from Theodotion.
It is also omitted by Lucifer 137, though there Lucifer omits
other verses as well. This quotation alone would not be enough
to shew that Lucifer used the shorter text; that he did so
however is clear from his long citations from Job xxi—xxvii at the
end of *De regibus apostaticis* (pp. 61 ff.). The Speculum (*m*) also
omits the Theodotion verses, though it shews here and there
signs of corruption from the Vulgate, the most startling being
Job xxxvi 13ᵃ in *m* 375. The Speculum text reappears in Priscillian, Job xl 3—9 being quoted by him (ed. p. 12) almost word
for word with *m* 436. The version used by Priscillian contained
the 'ridiculous name *Leusibora*' laughed at by S. Jerome (e.g. *Ep*
75 and *contra Vigilantium* § 7); that is to say, Job xxxviii 39ᵃ
θηρεύσεις δὲ λέουσι βοράν appears as '*tu capies Leosiboram*,' which
was supposed to refer to some monster. The 'Leosibora' is unknown
to the Egyptian versions, to Origen, and to the Greek Uncials,
which have the ν ἐφελκυστικὸν to λέουσι. It probably therefore
was a mistake of the original Latin translator, in whose copy the
ν must have been absent. In fact we do not meet with this Beast
except in the unrevised Old Latin; it occurs in none of the
Onomastica published by Lagarde.

2. That the verses derived from Theodotion were read by
S. Ambrose and S. Augustine is clear from Sabatier's notes to
Job xxi 23, xxiv 8ᵃ, xxvi 5—11, 14ᵃᵇ. All these verses are omitted

by the Thebaic and put under asterisks in the Hexaplar authorities (including S. Jerome's Latin version), but they are quoted by Ambrose and Augustine without suspicion.

3. S. Augustine's quotations generally agree verbally with S. Jerome. Those of S. Ambrose do not so agree. More definite proofs however are not wanting of the absolute independence of the latter.

Job v 23ª ὅτι μετὰ τῶν λίθων τοῦ ἀγροῦ ἡ διαθήκη σου LXX A.

These words are absent from the Thebaic and are under asterisks in all forms of the Hexapla. But for some reason they were not inserted like the other missing στίχοι in the common text, and so are absent from אB etc. (C is defective). It is therefore most important to notice that they are also omitted by Ambrose.

Job xxi 15 מַה שַׁדַּי] τί ἱκανός אABC.

This occurs in a passage under asterisk in the Hexapla. Here Ambrose ²/₂ has *quid prodest*, but Jerome *quid est Dominus*. Ἱκανός, as is well known, is the standing Greek rendering of 'Shaddai'.

Job xix 12. This passage exhibits in the clearest form the close connection of Augustine and Jerome, together with Ambrose's independence of them, while shewing at the same time that both have the interpolated verses.

Heb. יחד יבאו גדודיו ויסלו עלי דרכם ויחנו סביב לאהלי

LXX ὁμοθυμαδὸν δὲ ἦλθον τὰ πειρατήρια αὐτοῦ ἐπ᾽ ἐμοὶ ταῖς ὁδοῖς μου· ἐκύκλωσαν ἐνκάθητοι.

The division is that of א Theb. The translation is arrived at by omitting וַיָּסֹלּוּ and reading אָרְבִּי for the last word (cf. xxxi 9).

Ambrose :—*simul mihi uenerunt temptationes grauissimae circumdederunt me insidiantes.*

Jerome (following the Hexapla):—
 simul uenerunt temptationes eius
 **et fecerunt per me uiam suam*
 **et circumdederunt tabernaculum suum.*

The last of these clauses is quoted word for word by Augustine.

It is unfortunate that we have no decisive evidence as to the genuine O. L. rendering of πειρατήρια. In M. Berger's extracts from the margin of the *Codex Gothicus Legionensis* (Notices et Extraits, xxxiv, 2ᵐᵉ partie, p. 21) *pyratheria* occurs in Job x 17, but it is not absolutely clear that the whole of this interesting margin was not taken directly from a Greek MS[1]. The Thebaic takes the word in the sense of 'pirates' nests'.

4. I have not noticed any followers of S. Ambrose, but the later Africans are all like S. Augustine dependent on S. Jerome's version from the Hexapla. It will be enough here to refer to the crucial passages in Sabatier. For Vigilius of Tapsus they are Job xxvi 13 (*astra* Vig, corrupted from *claustra* Hier-Aug); xxviii 21; xxxvii 12ᵈ ([*in*] *gubernaculis* Vig-Hier-Aug = ἐν θεεβουλαθωθ Theod); xl 10—14. For Fulgentius we may refer to Job xiv 16, xxx 3 and xxxvi 10ᵇ, 11, and for Chromatius of Aquileia to xxxi 7—12ᵃ, 34ᵇ—39ᵃ. The *Opus Imperfectum in Mattheum* also had the interpolated στίχοι, as may be seen from Job xxxi 1 and xl 16.

---

[1] See pp. 9 and 10 of this Essay.

NOTE III.

On cod. Colbertinus (c).

The African character of the text of *c* at the end of S. Luke
is best exhibited by the comparison of a few verses with the
various European documents. The passage given below, Lc xxiv
36—end, was chosen as covering a quotation from Cypr. *Test* I 4
(Hartel, p. 43). In the left-hand column is given the text of *c*
with the variants of *e*, and Cyprian where extant; in the right-
hand column is the text of the Vulgate from Wordsworth and
White, with the variants of the chief European MSS *a b d ff* and *f*.
Italics in the left-hand column indicate where the 'African' authorities *c e Cyprian* differ among themselves; in the right-hand
column *italics* denote where more than one of the O. L. authorities
desert the Vulgate text. We may thus assume with comparative
certainty that the non-italic portions of each column give an African
and a European text respectively. For clearness, the points where
the Africans agree against all other authorities are printed in **bold-
face** type. No account is here taken of the orthography of *c*,
which is in the main that of an ordinary MS of the 12th cent.[1]

---

[1] Belsheim in the preface to his transcript of *c* gives as a specimen from
Mc xii 32: Un'÷W d̄s & n̄ ē ali' p̄t eū.

Lc xxiv 36—end

c	Vulgate
(with variants of *e* Cypr 43, bold-face type shewing agreement of the Africans against the rest. The brackets shew what I regard as comparatively late interpolations in the African base of *c*)	(with variants of *a b d ff f*)

³⁶haec **cum illi** loque**rentur**

ipse *dominus* stetit in medio
　　ipsorum

[*et dixit illis pax uobiscum*
　ego sum nolite timere]

³⁷**turb**ati autem et **in** timore
　　missi

puta**uerunt** se spiritum uidere

³⁸**ille autem** dixit illis quid tur-
　　bati estis

et quare cogitationes ascendunt
　in cor uestrum ?

---

³⁶*Dum* haec autem loqu*untur*

iesus stetit in medio eorum

et dicit eis pax uobis
　ego sum nolite timere

³⁷*conturbati uero* et conterriti

*existima*bant se spiritum uidere

³⁸*et* dixit *eis* quid turbati estis

et ∧ cogitationes ascendunt
　in cor*da* uestra ?

[Agreements of single 'European' MSS
　with the 'African' text given in small
　capitals]

---

36 dominus] *om. e*　　ipsorum] eorum
e　　et dixit...timere] *om. e*

37 timorem *e*

38 et] *om. e*

---

36 dum haec autem loq.]+ ILLI *b* ; et
dum h. loq. *a* ; haec autem eorum lo-
quentium *d* ; h. au. illis loquentibus *f*
iesus] ipse *a b d ff* ; ipse iesus *f*　　et
dicit...timere] *om. a b d ff*　　dixit *f* vg.
codd

37 cont. uero] exterriti autem *a* ;
conturbatique *b ff*　　ipsi autem
pauerunt *d*　　et TIMORE adprehensi
a ; et TIMORE tacti *d*　　putabant
se *a* ; putabant *d*　　spiritum] fan-
tasma *d*

38 qui dixit ILLIS *a* ; dixit autem ad
ILLOS *b ff* ; ad ille dixit ILLIS *d*　　quare
conturbati *d*　　et 2°]+quare *a b ff f* ;
+ut quid in *d* (sic)　　ascenderunt *ff*
corde uestro *a b ff* ; COR uestrum *d* ;
cordibus uestris *f*

[39]uidete manus meas et pedes
quoniam ego ipse sum
palpate et uidete *me quoniam*
spiritus
carnem et ossa non habet
sicut me uidetis habentem
[40][*et cum hoc dixisset*
ostendit eis manus et pedes]
[41]**cum** adhuc autem non crede-
rent
et *mirabantur* a gaudio
dixit **ad eos** *iesus*
habetis hic aliquid *quod* manducetur?
[42][*at illi obtulerunt ei*] partem
piscis assi
et porrexerunt *ei* et [*fauum mellis*]
[43]accepit coram illis
[*sumens reliquias dedit eis*]

[39]uidete manus meas et pedes ∧
quia ipse ego sum
palpate et uidete *quia* spiritus
carnem et ossa non habet
sicut me uidetis habere
[40]*et cum hoc dixisset*
ostendit eis manus et pedes.
[41]Adhuc autem *illis* non credentibus ∧
et mirantibus prae gaudio
dixit
habetis *hic* aliquid *quod* manducetur?
[42]at illi optulerunt ei partem
piscis assi
et fauum *mellis*
[43]*et cum* manducasset coram eis
sumens reliquias dedit eis.

39 me] *om. e*   quoniam 2°] quia *e*

40] *om. e*
41 crederent]+illi *e*   et cum ad-
mirarentur *e*   iesus] *om. e*   quod
mand.] manducare *e*

42 at illi obt. ei] *om. e*   et porr.
illi piscis assi partem *e*   fauum
mellis] *om. e*

43 sumens...eis] *om. e*

39 uidete]+ecce *b ff*   pedes]+meos
a b d ff   QUONIAM *a*   ego sum
ipse (*a*) *b ff f* (ipsi *a*); EGO IPSE sum *d*
palpate] tractate *a*   QUONIAM *a d*
ossum *a*   ossa n. h. nec carnes *d*
sicut]+et *d*   habeNTEM *a d*
40] *om. a b d ff*
41 non cred. illis *a* (*d*) *ff* (eis *d*)   et
mirant.] *post* gaudio *d f*   mirantibus]
stupentibus *a*; mirantibus *d*   ∧
gaudio *d*   dixit]+eis *f*   aliquid
quod edamus hic *a*; aliquid hic q.
mand. *b*; aliq. manducare hic *d*; hic
aliq. manducare *ff*
42 at illi] qui *a*; ET *d*   opt. (*uel*
obt.)] PORREXERUNT *a d*   ei] ILLI *a d*
piscis assi partem *a d*   assam *b*
et f. mellis] *om. d*; *om.* mellis *a b* (et de
fabo *b*)
43 cum...eis] ACCIPIENS manducauit
coram ILLIS *a* (*d*) (*f*) (accipiens in conspectu eorum manducauit *d*; accipiens
coram ipsis manducauit *f*); manducans
coram ipsis *b ff*   sumens...eis] *om.*
a b d ff

<table>
<tr><td>

⁴⁴et dixit *ad eos*
isti sermones *sunt* quos locutus
  sum ad uos
  cum adhuc essem uobiscum
quia oportet *impleri*
  omnia *quae* scripta *sunt*
in lege moysi et *in* prophetis
  et *in* psalmis de me
⁴⁵tunc *aperuit* illis sensum
  ut intellegerent scripturas
⁴⁶et dixit **illis**
quia scriptum est
  christum pati
et resurgere a mortuis
  tertia die
⁴⁷et praedicari in nomine eius
  paenitentiam
et remissa peccatorum
  usque in omnes gentes
incipiens ab hierusalem
⁴⁸et uos estis testes **eo**rum

</td><td>

⁴⁴*Et* dixit *ad eos*
haec *sunt* uerba quae locutus sum
  ad uos
  cum adhuc essem uobiscum
quoniam *necesse est* impleri
  omnia quae scripta sunt
in lege mosi et prophetis
  et psalmis de me
⁴⁵tunc aperuit illis sensum
  ut intellegerent *scripturas*
⁴⁶et dixit eis
quoniam sic scriptum est
et sic oportebat christum pati
et resurgere a mortuis
  die tertia ·
⁴⁷et praedicari in nomine eius
  paenitentiam
et remissionem peccatorum
  in omnes gentes
incipientibus ab *hierosolyma*
⁴⁸uos autem estis testes horum

</td></tr>
</table>

14 ad eos] illis *e*   isti] § *Cypr*
sunt sermones *Cypr*; *om.* sunt *e*   quia]
quoniam *e*   adimpleri *e Cypr*   quae
ser. sunt] scripta *Cypr*   in 2° et 3°]
om. e Cypr.

45 adaperuit *Cypr*

46

47 praedicare *e*   gentes] ¶ *Cypr*

48

44 et] *om.* b *ff*   eis *a d*   haec]
isti *d*   sunt] *om. a d*   SERMONES
mei QUOS *d*   ad uos] aput uos *a*;
om. vg. codd   adhuc] *om. d*   necesse est] OPORTET *a d*; oportuit *f*
suppleri *b*   moysi *a b ff f* vg. codd;
moysei *d*
45 adaperti sunt eorum sensus *d*
illis sensum] sensum illorum *a*   ad
intellegendum *a*; ut intellegant *d*
scripturas] ea quae scripta sunt *b ff*
46 QUIA sic scr. *d*   et sic oportebat]
et sic oportuit *f*; *om. a b d ff*   die
tertia] TERTIA DIE *a*; *om.* b *ff*
47 illius *a*   predicare *ff*   re-
missa *b*   in omn. gentibus *a*; in
omni gente *b ff*; super omnes gentes *d*
incipientibus] incipiens *a*; incipientium
d   hierusALEM *a d f*
48 ET uos autem *d* (*om.* estis)   testes
estis *ff*   horum] + omnium *f*

⁴⁹et ego mitto promissionem
  patris mei super uos
uos autem sedete in ciuitate
quoad usque indua**tis**
  uirtutem ex alto.
⁵⁰**Pro**duxit autem illos *foris*
  in bethania
et eleu**auit** manus suas
  et benedixit **illos**
⁵¹et factum est cum benedi**xisset**
  illos
  discessit ab *eis*
[*et ferebatur in caelum*]
⁵²et [*ipsi adorantes*] reuersi sunt *in*
  hierusalem cum gaudio magno
⁵³et *fuerunt* semper in templo
laudantes [*et benedicentes*] deum
  [*amen*].

⁴⁹et ego mitto promissum
  patris mei in uos
uos autem sedete in ciuita*te*
quoad usque induamini
  uirtutem *ex alto*.
⁵⁰Eduxit autem eos *foras*
  in bethaniam
et eleuatis manibus suis
  benedixit *eis*
⁵¹et factum est dum bene*diceret*
  illis
  recessit ab eis
et ferebatur in caelum
⁵²et ipsi *adorantes regressi* sunt in
  hierusalem cum gaudio magno
⁵³et erant semper in templo
laudantes *et benedicentes* deum
  amen.

49 patris mei] meam *c*   uos 2°]
illud *e* (sic)

50 illis *e*   foris] *om. c*   in]
quasi *e*   bethaniam *c*   lebabit *e*

51 -xissit *e*   ab illis *c*   et fer.
in cael.] *om. c*

52 ipsi adorantes] *om. e*   in]
om. e
   53 erant *e*   in templo semper *e*
et benedicentes] *om. c*   amen] *om. e*

49 et]+ecce *f*   mittam *a* vg.
codd   prom. pat. mei] repromissi-
onem patris *a*; promissa patris mei
b ff; promissionem meam *d*   in 1°]
super *a d*   ciuitate] ciuitatem *a ff*;
+hac hierusalem *f*   quoad usque]
donec *a*; usque dum *d*   ex alto] a
summo *a*; ab alto *b ff*; de alto *d*
   50 illos *a*; cum *ff*   foris *b ff*;
om. a   in] usque ad *a*; ad *d*
bethania *f*   et extollens manus suas
a; lebans autem manus *d*   suis]
om. ff   eis] eos *a b d ff f*
   51 dum] cum *d*   benedicit *b ff*
illos *a b ff*; eos *d f*   discessit *a d*
et fer. in cael.] *om. a b d ff*   ferebatur]
eleuabatur *f*
   52 adorantes] *om. a b d ff*; +eum *f*
reuersi *a d*
   53 conlaudantes *a*   et benedicentes]
om. a b d ff   deum] *om. b*   amen]
om. a b d ff vg. codd

The words bracketed in vv. 36, 40, 42, 43 and 51—53 are
instances of what I venture to consider interpolations in c from the

Vulgate. It will be noticed that apart from these bracketed passages the text of *c* is quite of a different type from that of the Vulgate. It will also be noticed that the 'African' text of *c e* Cypr is not unfrequently supported by single MSS of the 'European' type; this is especially the case with *a* and *d*. But there remain eighteen readings in the thirteen verses where *c e* (with Cyprian where extant) are agreed against all the other Latin texts. These are the readings printed in the left-hand column in bold-face type, and they are sufficient both in number and character to prove that in this passage *c* has a fundamentally 'African' text. The reading *quia scriptum est* in *ver.* 46 is especially noteworthy, in the first place because *c e* and Cyprian join in omitting *sic* against every known authority, both Greek and Latin, and again because they join (with *d*) in reading *quia* for *quoniam*, although the 'African' text often has *quoniam* where the others have *quia*.

The text of *c* contains a valuable 'African' element elsewhere than in the later chapters of S. Luke. Examples may be found for instance in Mc xii 22, 40. In many parts of the Gospels on the other hand *c* sides rather with the ordinary 'European' Old Latin than with *k* or *e*. But in any case African texts are so uncommon, that the smallest fragment is of great value to the textual critic; and my object in writing this Note is not so much to investigate the composition of *c*, as to draw attention to the fact that there is in it a genuine African strain of good quality and of considerable extent.

Tabulated Renderings.

[In the following tables the chief O. Lat. MSS are quoted wherever available, so that silence may be taken to mean that a MS is not extant at that point.]

1. εἰ δὲ μή [γε]

	si quo minus	alioquin	sin autem	(other renderings)
Mt vi 1	k	a bd c f vg Chrom		ne f Aug, om. e
ix 17	k	a bdhc f vg		ne f
Mc ii 21		a bd ffirq vg Faust	c	
22		e a bd cffirq vg		
Lc v 36	e dc	a b ff rq f vg		
37	e dc	a b ff rq f vg		
x 6	e dc Aug		ab rq f vg	
xiii 9	e d		b cffi qf vg Amb$^{3}/_{3}$	{ ceteroquin a / sin autem minus Aug
xiv 32	d	a b ff rq vg Aug$^{1}/_{2}$	d r	{ ceterum e Aug$^{1}/_{2}$ / si autem impossibilis est f
Joh xiv 2	ebdeff vg	a rq f		Hil$^{2}/_{2}$ uel q
11	e (m) (Tert)	(a)b ff (f) vg Amb	d r	

The bracketed authorities in Joh xiv 11 add *uel* to the rendering under which they are quoted.

What is especially noteworthy in the above table is the way in which the African text is entirely unaffected by the great shifting of the European attestation in Lc x 6 and xiii 9 from *alioquin* to *sin autem*. No more decisive proof of the essential unity of the European texts could be given. A similar case will be found in Mt xxiv 21 under ὁ κόσμος.

2. παραβολή		similitudo		parabola
Mt xiii 3—36	$k^{11}/_{11}$			$e^{9}/_{9}\,abd\,\&c.^{11}/_{11}$
(*eleven* times)				
53	k e			abd ,,
xv 15	e	corb		a d ,,
xxi 33				e abd ,,
45				e abd ,,
xxii 1				e abd ,,
xxiv 32	e	Aug$^{1}/_{2}$		abd ,,
Mc iii 23				e abd ,,
iv 2		b		e a d ,,
10		b		a d ,,
11			Sina et Sion § 1	abd ,,
13		b		a d ,,
13		b		a d ,,
30		b		e d ,,
33				e bd ,,
34		(om. e)		bd ,,
vii 17		an		bd ,,
xii 1	k			bd ,,
12	k			abd ,,
xiii 28	k a			d ,,

N.B. In an interpolation prefixed to Mt xiii 44 *b* has 'similitudo'.

Before proceeding to the evidence from S. Luke we may notice that *similitudo* seems thoroughly African. It is found in *k* wherever extant, and though *e* here often joins the European array, the African character of the word is vindicated by its occurrence in the tract *De montibus Sina et Sion*. On the other hand *parabola* is always found in *f* vg, though here and there the best European MSS have singly *similitudo*.

		similitudo		parabola
Lc	iv 23	*c*	*beff rqf* vg	*a d*
	v 36	*c*	*b ff q* vg *Amb*	*a dc r f*
	vi 39	*c*	*b ff rqf* vg *Aug*	*a dc*
	viii 4	*c*	*b ff rqf* vg	*a dc*
	9	*c*	*r*	*abdeff qf* vg
	10	*e*		*abdeff rqf* vg
	11	*c*	*r* (*Tert*)	*abdeff qf* vg
	xii 16	*em b ffirqf* vg		*a dc* (*Tert*)
	41	*c*	*b ffi q*	*dc r f* vg
	xiii 6	*c*	*beffirqf* vg	*a d*
	xiv 7	*e*	*q* (*om. b*)	*a deffir f* vg
	xv 3	*c*	*beffi q*	*a d f* vg
	xviii 1	*e*		*abdeffirqf* vg *Tert*
	9	*c*	*beffirq Opt Aug*	*a f* vg (*om. d*)
	xix 11	*e*	*sbeffirq*	*a d f* vg
	xx 9	*c*		*a deffirqf* vg
	19	*e*	*eff rq* vg	*a d i f*
	xxi 29	*c*	*effir f* vg	*a d q*

N.B. παροιμία = *prouerbium* (Joh x 6; xvi 25 *bis*, 29), but *similitudo* occurs in Joh xvi 25 *bis a Aug*; 29 *e a*.

It is obvious that the balance of evidence is here much disturbed, many European documents supporting *similitudo* against *parabola*. What is of great importance to note is that when *b* has 'similitudo' (which the analogy of the other Gospels would lead us to suppose was the original rendering), some but not all the MSS retain the word also. On the other hand, when *b* has the non-African word 'parabola' *it carries with it all the European* MSS. The only exception is the reading of *r* in Lc viii 9, 11, which may be due to mechanical assimilation to viii 4. So far therefore as the criticism of this single word takes us, *b* seems to represent an eclectic stage of the European text which was the ultimate foundation of the later revisions such as *ff*, *f*, and so of the Vulgate.

3. [ὁ] κόσμος. This word occurs 95 times in the four Gospels. The chief facts about the three Latin renderings *mundus*, *orbis* [*terrae*], and *saeculum*, are given below.

(i) *Mundus* is by far the most common except in the African text of S. John, and is found there also when any interpretation but the physical world is excluded, e.g. in the last verse of the Gospel.

(ii) *Orbis* (or *orbis terrae*, or *o. terrarum*) is the regular Latin equivalent of ἡ οἰκουμένη[1]. As a rendering of κόσμος it occurs as follows:

> in Mt:—iv 8 *Hil* (*o. terrarum*, from Lc iv 5); xvi 26 *de laud. mart*; xxvi 13 *h* and Wordsworth's British MSS QR.
>
> in Lc:—ix 25 *sess* [but 'mundus' Cypr. *Test* III 61 codd. opt]
>
> in Joh:—never

but in Mc:—viii 36 *c d* ['mundus' *k b rell.*; 'sacculum' *a n*]
xiv 9 *c* (*k*) ['orbis terrae' *k*; 'mundus' *a rell.*]
xvi 15 *c o q Amb* ['mundus' *ff* vg]

In xvi 15 the attestation includes most of the extant O. L. evidence; *o* is the supplementary last leaf of *n*. The evidence of *sess* in Lc ix 25 suggests that *orbis* is sometimes a late African substitution for *mundus*. In the addition to *k* Mc xvi 4 *orbis terrae* probably stands for ἡ οἰκουμένη not ὁ κόσμος[2].

(iii) *Saeculum* is the regular equivalent for αἰών in all Latin texts[3], but as a rendering of κόσμος it is never found in the African text of Mt Mc and Lc. Even in Mt xxiv 21 *e* and Cyprian have *mundus*, though all the good European MSS have *saeculum*.

In European texts of Mt Mc Lc *saeculum* (= κόσμος) occurs

> Mt xiii 38 *d Iren*
> Mc viii 36 *a n*
> Lc xii 30 *a*

and for ἀπ᾽ ἀρχῆς κόσμου Mt xxiv 21 we find

> *ab initio saeculi* in *a b d h c ff r q corb* Wordsworth's ER and *Iren*.

This affords by the way a striking instance of the 'European' character of *Iren.*lat. The allied phrase ἀπὸ καταβολῆς κόσμου

---

[1] In the four passages from the Gospels where ἡ οἰκουμένη occurs the only exceptions I know are that in Mt xxiv 14 *d* and Wordsworth's E have *mundus*, and that in Lc iv 5 D^{gr} has τοῦ κόσμου for τῆς οἰκουμένης followed by *d* and by *f*.

[2] Cf. *Anaph. Pilati* (Tisch. ed. 2, p. 446).

[3] A partial exception is formed by phrases meaning 'for ever' (εἰς τὸν αἰῶνα, etc.), where *in aeternum* and *in aeuum* occur. *In perpetuum* is also occasionally found.

(Mt xiii 38) is also rendered *ab initio saeculi* in *d h*, but *a constitutione mundi* in *a b c ff q f* vg *Hil* and *ab origine* in *k e*, the two African MSS omitting κόσμου with the true Greek text.

On the other hand *saeculum* is the characteristic African rendering for κόσμος in S. John, the European documents having generally *hic mundus*, corrected in the Vulgate to *mundus* alone.

In documents not predominantly African *saeculum* occurs

Joh iv 42	*q*	[= *e*]
vi 14	*d*	[*e* om. ver]
33	*q*	[= *e*; *q* has *hoc saec.*]
51	*q*	[= *e Cypr Aug*; against *Tert*]
ix 5	*d*	[= *e*]
xii 46	*Aug*	[against *e*]
xiv 30	*Hil¹*/₄	[= *e*]
xv 18, 19 (*sexies*)	*r*	[= *e Cypr²*/₃; against *Cypr¹*/₃]
xvi 28	*r*	[= *e*]
33ᵈ	*r Hil*	[= *e Cypr²*/₃; against *Cypr¹*/₃]
xvii 6	*r Hil*	[= *e*]
9	*r*	[= *e*]
xviii 36 (*bis*)	*Hil*	[= *e Cypr*]

i.e. instances are only found in 14 verses out of 58 in which κόσμος occurs.

With regard to the variation of rendering in *e* it may be remarked that in addition to Joh xvii 5, 24, and xxi 25, where ὁ κόσμος means the whole creation and consequently *mundus* is alone appropriate, *mundus* not *saeculum* is found in *e* from Joh i 1—iii 17ᵃ (seven times), x 36—xii 46 (eight times), xvi 11, and xvii 25. In the last of these passages it is probably the result of mechanical assimilation to the preceding verse. But though the change from *saeculum* to *mundus* in x 36—xii 46 is decisively not confirmed by S. Cyprian's quotations, the use of *mundus* in chap. i is confirmed, as in all five places S. Cyprian also has *mundus* not *saeculum*. It is possible therefore that the original African translator started the Gospel with *mundus*, but changed the rendering later on to *saeculum*, from a sense perhaps of the close relation in which the Johannine κόσμος stands to the αἰών of the Synoptists.

NOTE V.

On the 'Western' Interpolations in the Gospels.

The main object of this Note is to bring together those *additions* to the Gospels, which from the novelty of their contents might be held to indicate the use of independent sources for the enrichment of the narrative by 'Western' scribes. The passages are assumed to be no part of the original text on the authority of B and its allies, which with a few exceptions omit them all. By exhibiting the early attestation of these Interpolations in a tabular form we gain some idea of how far they are supported *as a body* by the 'African' or the 'European' groups of the Old Latin, or again by the Old Syriac; we may even by this means gain some idea of their local origin.

No account is here taken of mere harmonistic additions, nor of variations which can plausibly be assigned to palaeographical error. The passages chosen have been divided into two classes. Those in Table A are the longer Interpolations, each containing a sentence complete in itself; some indeed are complete narratives. They have been arranged in what has seemed to the present writer their degree of independence of the true text. They begin with the wholly new narrative of the Woman taken in Adultery, a narrative not even suggested by the context in which it now occurs; and they end with adaptations of words found elsewhere in the Gospels (Nos. 13—16), which are distinguished from the class of harmonistic additions by the peculiar context in which they are introduced, whereby a new turn is given to the words. The passages given in Table B are mere expansions of the Evangelical text; they are mostly very short, and rarely contain a verb except in a dependent clause.

The very general absence of these Interpolations from the Sinai Palimpsest (syr. *sin*) might seem to suggest that an ancestor of that MS had been corrected to the ℵB text by *excision*. I have therefore added in a separate Table the Interpolations of the same internal character as those in Tables A and B which are found in syr. *sin* or syr. *crt*, but not in the earlier forms of the Latin. Had the ancestors of syr. *sin* really suffered mutilation, these passages would have been cut out with the others. The fact that these interpolations are found in syr. *sin* makes it less probable that its ancestors ever contained the passages collected in Table A.

In the following Tables the critical symbol for a MS indicates that the MS in question contains such and such a reading; 'om.' indicates that it omits the reading; '—' indicates that it is not extant at the point. Where *a* is missing I have given the reading of the kindred MS *n*.

A.   *The Greater Interpolations and their Western Attestation.*

Manuscripts quoted	D	lat. afr			lat. eur		syr. vt		'Received Text'
		k	Cypr	e	a (or n)	b	crt	sin	
1. Joh vii 53–viii 11 (The Woman taken in Adultery)	D	—		e	om.	b*	om.	om.	ς
2. Le vi 5 (The Man working on the Sabbath)	D	—		om.	om.	om.	—	—	om.
3. Mt iii 15 *fin.* (The Light at the Baptism)	om.	—		—	a	om.	om.	om.	om.
4. Mc xvi 3 (The Light at the Resurrection)	om.	k		—	— [om. n] —		—	om.	om.
5. Le xxii 43, 44 (The Bloody Sweat)	D	—		e	a	b	crt	om.	ς
6. Le xxiii 34ᵃ ("Father, forgive them")	om.	—		e	om.	om.	crt	om.	ς
7. Joh v 4 (The Angel at the Pool)	om.	—		e	a	b	om.	—	ς
8. Mt xvi 2ᵇ, 3 ("The Face of the Sky")	D	—		e	a	b	om.	om.	ς
9. Mt xx 28 *fin.* ("Seek from little to increase")	D	—		e	a	b	crt	[om.]	om.
10. Le ix 55 ("Ye know not what spirit ye are of......but to save them")	(D)	— Cypr	e	a	b	crt	om.	ς
11. Mc xii 22, 23 ("To whom is the woman clean")	om.	k		—	om.	om.	—	om.	om.

Manuscripts quoted	D	lat. afr			lat. eur		syr. vt		'Received Text'
		k	Cypr	e	a	b	crt	sin	
12. Lc xxiii 2, 5 ("Loosing the Law...") ("our sons and wives...")	om.	—		e	om.	(b)	om.	om.	om.
13. Lc xxiii 53 (The great Stone)	D	—		om.	om.	om.	om.	om.	om.
14. Mt xviii 11 (" To save the lost ")	D	—		om.	a	b	crt	om.	𝕾
15[1]. Mt xx 16[b] (" Many are called ")	D	—		e	a	b	crt	sin	𝕾
16. Mc xiii 2 fin. (" Another made without hands ")	D	k	Cypr	e	a	b	—	om.	om.
17. Joh iii 6 (" For God is a Spirit ")	—	— (? om. Cypr)		e	a	om.	crt	sin	om.
18. Joh vi 56 (" The Body of the Son of Man as the Bread of Life ")	D	—		om.	a	om.	om.	om.	om.

The merest glance at the above Table is enough to shew that the important additions to the Gospel narrative here collected together are thoroughly characteristic of the African text. Of the 18 passages only four are rejected by any extant African authority[2], and of these four it is quite doubtful whether No. 14 should not have been excluded from this list as a harmonistic addition, while No. 18 may be regarded as a mere adaptation from the context. The only one of the more important Interpolations actually omitted in the extant fragments of e or k is the famous story of the Man working on the Sabbath, which appears at Lc vi 5 in Codex Bezae only. Here however k, the better African MS, is missing. Nos. 12 and 13 are also found in c, a MS which in this chapter has a fundamentally African text.

It is worth while pointing out also that neither k nor e is extant for Mt iii 15. The story of the Fire on Jordan at the

---

[1] To No. 15 perhaps should be added Mc vii 16 ("He that hath ears to hear"), which is found in syr. sin as well as 𝕾 D a b (hiant e k).

[2] An apparent exception is Joh iii 6 (No. 17), a verse twice quoted by S. Cyprian without the final addition "For God is a Spirit," but as he does not go on to quote ver. 7 it cannot be proved that the clause was not in his Bible. The verse was quoted with the additional clause by S. Cyprian's suffragan Nemesianus of Thubunae at the Council of Carthage.

Baptism (No. 3) is now only found in *a* among the older texts, being omitted by D *b* and syr. vt. It is clearly analogous to the story of the Light at the Resurrection, preserved only in *k* (Mc xvi 4, No. 4); *a* has a large element akin to the African text, and it is probable that it derived this interpolation from that element. We may even conjecture that the passage had a place in the missing leaf of *k*. In other words the interpolation is not unlikely to have had the same origin as the rest of those in Table A.

The absence of several of the most characteristic of these passages from the European Latin MSS, and also from the bilingual Codex Bezae, seems to shew the sobering influence of later Greek texts.

This Table moreover affords one of many indications that syr. crt has been partially revised from the Greek. Most of the interpolations it has accepted are those found also in the *Textus Receptus*, i.e. interpolations which had a wide circulation in the East at the beginning of the 4th cent. The presence of the long interpolation after Mt xx 28 in the Greek Uncial Φ and in syr. hl. mg proves that this passage also was not unknown in later times in the East, though it was not taken up into the Antiochian text. No stress can therefore be laid on its presence in syr. crt as a proof of special affinity with the older forms of the Latin.

I have not inserted the 'Longer Conclusion' to S. Mark in this list, from which it differs entirely in character. In the first place it is a supplement to an imperfect document[1], not an interpolation into a text complete without it. Again, in internal character it is more like a narrative freely compiled from Lc and Mt than the quite independent stories that stand at the head of Table A; [Mc] xvi 9—20 indeed contains hardly a detail of fact which is not found elsewhere in the Gospels or Acts. It is therefore of the highest importance from the point of view of Textual Criticism to observe that the attestation of the 'Longer Conclusion' differs in a vital point from that of the passages in Table A. Codd. *a* and *b* are unfortunately missing here, but the verses are found in D and in *n*, a MS closely resembling *a* in

---

[1] In no case would the Gospel have *originally* ended with ἐφοβοῦντο γάρ. Ought we not indeed to print ἐφοβοῦντο γάρ...˙ with a grave accent? It is very unusual to find clauses, much less paragraphs, which end with γάρ. Cf. Mc xi 18 and ix 6.

S. Mark; there is therefore no doubt that they are part of the European Latin text. But they are absent from *k*. In their place *k* has the well-known 'Shorter Conclusion', which is found also in L and other later Egyptian texts as an alternative. In its independence of the genuine text of the New Testament the 'Shorter Conclusion' resembles the more characteristic passages in Table A, and seems to me not improbably to belong to the same stratum of interpolation, i.e. to be bound up with the history of the African Latin.

B. *The Smaller Interpolations and their Western Attestation.*

Manuscripts quoted	D	lat. afr			lat. eur		syr. vt		'Received Text'
		k	Cypr	e	a	b	crt	sin	
1. Mt vii 21 *fin.*] + οὗτος εἰσελεύσεται εἰς τὴν βασιλείαν τῶν οὐρανῶν	—	k	Cypr	—	a	b	crt	—	om.
2. Mt x 23 φεύγετε εἰς τὴν ἑτέραν] + κἂν ἐκ ταύτης διώκωσιν ὑμᾶς, φεύγετε εἰς τὴν ἄλλην	D	k	—		a	b	—	sin	om.
3. Mt xxv 1 τοῦ νυμφίου] + καὶ τῆς νύμφης	D	—			a	b	—	sin	om.
4. Mc iii 32 οἱ ἀδελφοί σου] + καὶ αἱ ἀδελφαί σου	D	—	om.		a	b	—	?	om.
5. Mc iv 9 ἀκουέτω] + καὶ ὁ συνίων συνιέτω	D	—	—		a	b	—	om.	om.
6. Mc v 33 τρέμουσα] + διὸ πεποιήκει λάθρᾳ	D	—	om.		a	om.	—	—	om.
7. Mc vii 4 χαλκίων] + καὶ κλινῶν	D	—	—		a	b	—	om.	ς
8. Mc vii 13 τῇ παραδόσει ὑμῶν] + τῇ μωρᾷ	D	—	—		a	b	—	om.	om.
9. Mc ix 24 παιδίου] + μετὰ δακρύων	D	om.	—		a	b	—	om.	ς
10. Mc ix 29 προσευχῇ] + καὶ νηστείᾳ	D	om.	—		a	b	—	(sin)	ς
11. Mc x 22 κτήματα πολλά] + καὶ ἀγρούς	om.	k	—		om.	b	—	om.	om.
12. Mc x 24 δύσκολόν ἐστιν] + τοὺς πεποιθότας ἐπὶ (τοῖς) χρήμασιν	D	om.	—		a	b	—	sin	ς
13. Mc xii 40 χηρῶν] + καὶ ὀρφανῶν	D	om.	om		a	b	—	om.	om.
14. Mc xiv 68 *fin.*] + καὶ ἀλέκτωρ ἐφώνησεν	D	k			a	–	—	om.	ς

Manuscripts quoted	D	lat. afr			lat. eur		syr. vt		'Received Text'
		k	Cypr	e	a	b	crt	sin	
15. Lc i 28 *fin.*]+ εὐλογημένη σὺ ἐν γυναιξίν	D	—		e	a	b	—	—	ς
16. Lc vi 1 ἐν σαββάτῳ]+δευτεροπρώτῳ	D	—		(e)	a	om.	—	—	ς
17. Lc vi 17 Ἰερουσαλήμ] + καὶ Πεδαίας	(?)	—		om.	a	b	—	om.	om.
18. Lc ix 54 ἀναλῶσαι αὐτούς]+ ὡς καὶ Ἡλείας ἐποίησεν	D	—		om.	a	b	om.	om.	ς
19. Lc xvii 11 Γαλιλαίας] + *et Hiericho*	om.	—		e	a	b	crt	om.	om.
20. Lc xx 34 οἱ υἱοί...τούτου]+ γεννῶνται καὶ γεννῶσιν	D	—		(c)	a	—	crt	sin	om.
21. Lc xxi 11 ἔσται]+ *et hiemes*	om.	—		om.	a	—	crt	om.	om.
22. Lc xxii 68 οὐ μὴ ἀποκριθῆτε] + ἢ ἀπολύσητε	D	—		(e)	a	b	crt	sin	ς
23. Lc xxiv 42 ἰχθύος ὀπτοῦ μέρος] + καὶ ἀπὸ μελισσίου κηρίον (*v.* κηρίου)	D	—		om.	a	b	crt	om.	ς
24. Joh iii 6 σάρξ ἐστιν]+ὅτι ἐκ τῆς σαρκὸς ἐγεννήθη	—	—		e	a	b	crt	om.	om.
25. Joh iii 8 ἐκ]+τοῦ ὕδατος καὶ	—	—		e	a	b	crt	sin	om.
26. Joh iii 13 τοῦ ἀνθρώπου]+ὁ ὢν ἐν τῷ οὐρανῷ	—	—		(e)	a	b	(crt)	(sin)	ς
27. Joh v 3ª ξηρῶν]+παραλυτικῶν	—	—		om.	a	b	om.	—	om.
28. Joh v 3ᵇ ἐκδεχομένων τὴν τοῦ ὕδατος κίνησιν	D	—		e	a	b	om.	—	ς
29. Joh vi 59 Καφαρναούμ]+σαββάτῳ	D	—		om.	a	om.	om.	om.	om.

The difference of character between the passages in Tables A and B is paralleled by the difference between their attestation. In Table A the passages were most steadily supported by the African text, while they were almost wholly absent from the earlier form of the Old Syriac as represented by syr. *sin*. The more modest interpolations comprised in Table B are regularly found only in the European Latin. Some of them appear also in syr. *sin*, but on the other hand about half are absent from the African Latin. No. 14 might perhaps have been placed in Table A.

It is worth noting that subsidiary glosses are now and then found in the European Latin in the immediate neighbourhood of the more important interpolations given under Table A. Instances are Lc ix 54, Joh iii 6 and v 3.

Some few of these 'interpolations' may possibly not be interpolations at all, but portions of the true text which have fallen out in אB. This is especially the case with the addition in Mt x 23, which may be held to improve the run of the sentence; the longer reading here has moreover very considerable Greek support in addition to lat. afr-eur and syr. vt. Almost as much may be said for the addition to Mt xxv 1, though at this point it is more difficult to see how the words 'and the bride' could have dropped out, on the supposition that they are genuine.

The general impression left on my mind by Tables A and B may be expressed as follows. (1) The earliest Latin version contained a text of the Gospels enriched by additions, some of which go far beyond the mere inventiveness of scribes, and must ultimately have been derived from independent historical sources. In this respect the African text has most faithfully preserved the original Latin version. (2) Another series of interpolations of a less bold type is especially characteristic of the European Latin. This series is less certainly based on independent sources and seems to be of later origin, though from the comparatively small scale of each addition they were easily introduced into MSS and so are widely spread among various types of text. The comparative isolation of the African text, which has preserved the longer interpolations, has kept that text more free from these lesser interpolations than any other predominantly 'Western' text. (3) The eclectic texts of the 4th cent. in various languages took up a certain number of both classes of interpolations, some of them even finding a place in the great Vulgates of later times.

C. *Greater Interpolations characteristic of the Old Syriac.*

1. Mt iv 9 καὶ εἶπεν αὐτῷ] + '*These kingdoms and their glory hast thou seen?*'　　　　　　　　　　　　　　　　　　syr. *sin* [om. *crt*]

2. Mt xxvii 16, 17 '*Jesus* Barabbas'　　　　　　　　　　syr. *sin*

3. Mc xii 23 ἐν τῇ ἀναστάσει] + οὖν ὅταν ἀναστῶσιν　　syr. *sin*

4. Mc xiii 8 λιμοί] + καὶ ταραχαί   syr. *sin*

5. Lc xxiii 48 *fin.*] + 'and saying : *Woe to us! what has befallen us? Woe to us from our sins!*'   syr. *sin-crt*

6. Joh xi 39 Κύριε,]+'*why are they taking away the stone?*' syr.*sin*

7. Joh xii 12 τῇ ἐπαύριον] + 'he went out and came to the Mount of Olives'   syr. *sin*

8. Joh xx 16 διδάσκαλε] + καὶ προσέδραμεν ἅψασθαι αὐτοῦ   syr. *sin*

Except in Nos. 1 and 5 syr. *crt* is missing, but to Lc xxiii 43 syr. *crt* adds καὶ λαβὼν τὰ ἐπίλοιπα ἔδωκεν αὐτοῖς with the later Syriac and Latin versions (including lat. vg) as well as some Gk mss, but not syr. *sin* nor D *a b e*; in fact, this gloss is found in no document which does not also contain the clause about the honey-comb.

The Greek and Latin attestation of these additions is as follows. Nos. 1, 6 and 7 are unsupported. No. 2 was known to Origen and is found in the group of cursives 1-118-209. No. 3 is in ϛ and late Gk mss generally; in Latin it is found in *a* (*b*) *ff i q* and vg. No. 4 is also in ϛ, but the Latin attestation is confined to *q*. No. 5 appears to be alluded to in *Evang. Petri* § 7, and is found with an extra clause in the late and professedly eclectic ms *g*[1]. It is a natural conjecture that *g*[1] derived it from some Latin form of the Diatessaron. No. 8 is found in אᶜᵃ, as well as in *g*[1] *gat* and Wordsworth's DE. (It will be remembered that *g*[1] is Wordsworth's G in Mc Lc and Joh; Westcott and Hort call it *ger.* Wordsworth's E used to be called *mm.*)

This list of interpolations found in syr. vt, but not the older Latin texts, would have been somewhat enlarged if account had been taken of the 'Non-Western Interpolations'. Many of these passages are omitted by syr. vt, but some are retained, although the balance of internal evidence is decidedly against them. A notable instance is Lc xxiv 12, omitted by D lat. vt, but found in syr. *sin-crt* as well as אBϛ.

Presbyter quoque Hieronymvs trium linguarum peritus ex Hebraeo in Latinum eloquium easdem Scripturas conuertit eloquenterque transfudit, cvivs Interpretatio merito ceteris antefertvr; nam est et verborvm tenacior et perspicvitate sententiae clarior, atque utpote a Christiano interprete uerior.

The first half of this statement was taken by S. Isidore from Aug. *de Ciuitate Dei* xviii 43; the second half is an adaptation of *de Doctrina Christiana* ii 22.

THE 'ITALA'.

THE non-African texts of the Old Latin were divided by Dr Hort into sub-families, 'European' and 'Italian', the latter term being defined as the text used by S. Augustine and praised by him under the name of *Itala*. The object of the following Essay is to shew that the text of the Gospels found in S. Augustine's later works is not an 'Old Latin' text at all, but the Vulgate itself, and that this was the *Itala* commended by him in the famous passage of the *de Doctrina Christiana*.

Dr Hort assigned the Gospel MSS *f* (Brixianus) and *q* (Monacensis) to the 'Italian' family (*Introd.* §§ 110, 111). These codices differ from almost all the other Old Latin MSS in containing many Antiochian readings, and it is undeniable that S. Augustine's quotations also contain many such readings[1]. But the same is true of the Vulgate; it is therefore necessary to look more minutely at the various texts to ascertain their mutual relations. For the sake of convenience I shall speak of the Revised Version of S. Jerome as the Vulgate, although in the fourth and fifth centuries the name was not uncommonly used for what is now called the 'Old Latin'.

As soon as the Latinity of the 'Italian' group is studied without special reference to the type of Greek text represented by the various MSS, it becomes at once evident that Dr Hort's classification is unsatisfactory. The first blow to it was dealt by Mr White

---

[1] Scrivener's *Introduction* (ed. 4, vol. ii, p. 350) thus adduces the testimony of S. Augustine to support the Received Text of Lc x 41, 42: "His Old Latin copies, at any rate, contained the words '...porro unum est necessarium...'". *Now* 'porro' *never occurs in the Old Latin Gospels.* It is found in the Vulgate in the three places Mt viii 27, Lc x 42 and xi 20, but never in a single Old Latin MS, *sed* or *autem* being used instead. This instance alone would make the use of the Vulgate by S. Augustine highly probable.

in his edition of *q* (*Old Latin Bibl. Texts*, iii). In that work he shewed that, although *f* and *q* have a good many readings in common that affect the underlying Greek text (mostly of an Antiochian type), their renderings of Greek words are often quite different, *f* as a rule agreeing with the Vulgate and *q* with *b*. This, I may add, is not due to the intrusion of a Vulgate element in *f*. The more that MS is studied the more evident appears the probability of the common opinion, that *f* is an example of the type of text from which S. Jerome prepared his Revised Version. But neither the renderings found in *f*, nor those in *q*, nor those found in both combined, agree especially with those of S. Augustine's quotations, except where they also agree with the Vulgate[1].

What then was the text actually used by S. Augustine?

To reconstruct S. Augustine's Bible is a task of much difficulty. In the first place it is most important to separate off the quotations made by S. Augustine at first hand from the Bible from those which he makes in quoting the works of others. In the latter case he keeps to the Biblical text used by the person from whom he is quoting. A good instance is *de Doct. Christ.* iii 30 ff., where more than twenty verses of the Bible are quoted accurately from Tyconius, though Tyconius's own words are paraphrased.

Not less necessary is it to note the date of each treatise. In some of S. Augustine's earlier works, as for instance the *contra Faustum*, the old African text is clearly visible even in the quotations from the Gospel. Thus to render οἰνοπότης, 'wine-bibber', in Mt xi 19 (Lc vii 34) we have

'potator' *a b q* (Mt)	but 'uinaria' *k* Aug$^2/_3$ (Mt)
'potator uini' *c f* vg (Mt)	'uinarius' *e r* (Lc)
'uini potator' *d h* (Mt); *c d l* (Lc)	
	('uinosus' Aug$^1/_3$ *Epp*; Aug
'bibens uinum' *a b ff q f* vg (Lc)	*de bono coniug* has 'uinaria'
	codd. opt, but 'uinarius' *codd*,
	'potator uini' *codd*)

Here we see how the rare word *uinaria*, preserved in the African authorities, has been variously improved away in the other MSS, while S. Augustine himself once substitutes *uinosus*. 'Africanisms

---

[1] See the Note on the text of the *de Consensu* for an example.

of this kind are rare in his later writings, though not entirely absent in the case of quotations made from memory.

The three works of S. Augustine which will come under immediate consideration in this Essay were written in the few years preceding and following 400 AD. The mention of the *Itala* occurs in the first edition of *de Doctrina Christiana*, issued in 397 AD, and the *Acta contra Felicem* date from 404. At some date between these limits comes the publication of *de Consensu Euangelistarum*. It may be convenient here to remind ourselves that the Vulgate Gospels were issued in 384, the rest of the Bible following at intervals till about 405, so that when S. Augustine was writing the *de Doctrina Christiana* the portions of S. Jerome's version actually published were the N. Test., Sam. and Kings, Ezr. and Nehem., and the sixteen Prophets.

S. Augustine's relations with the Vulgate have not, I venture to think, been properly understood. It will indeed be acknowledged by all that to the end of his days in short easily remembered phrases from the Gospel S. Augustine often used the Old Latin. In other words, there is no doubt that in the kind of quotation where it is least likely that a writer would look the passage up in his Codex he used the type of text current in his younger days. But what I believe has not received sufficient attention is the remarkable extant evidence tending to shew that during S. Augustine's episcopate, from about 400 AD onwards, the Church at Hippo read the Gospels from S. Jerome's version, though for the Acts it retained a very pure form of the Old African Latin.

The evidence is as follows. In AD 404 a Manichee preacher named Felix appeared at Hippo, where he was arrested and brought to trial before the ecclesiastical courts. This trial is reported at length in the tract called *Acta contra Felicem Manichaeum* (or Aug. *contra Felicem*). The statements of Felix about the coming of the Holy Spirit had been so unsatisfactory that S. Augustine determined to read to him the full Biblical account. Accordingly a codex of the Gospels was handed to him and he read from it to Felix Lc xxiv 36—49. Having read these verses he gave back the book of the Gospels and was then handed a codex of the Acts, from which he read the whole of the first chapter and the first eleven verses of the second. What S. Augustine read out is given *in*

extenso in our MSS of Aug. *contra Felicem,* and an examination of the
two passages leads to the surprising result that the passage from
S. Luke is pure Vulgate, while the text of the Acts is that of S.
Cyprian—the very oldest form of the African version known to us.
This very remarkable state of things cannot very well be the result
of corruption in our MSS of Aug. *contra Felicem,* for had the Gospel
passage been corrected wholesale to the Vulgate, it is difficult to
see why the still longer passage from the Acts should have wholly
escaped.   We cannot therefore but conclude that the codex of the
Gospels handed to S. Augustine was a Vulgate codex, and the
codex of the Acts was an Old Latin codex containing an ' African '
text—in other words, that by 404 AD the Gospels were read at
Hippo from the Vulgate, while in some other books of the Bible,
such as the Acts, the unrevised Old Latin was still publicly used[1].

To such a composite late African New Testament belongs the
Fleury Palimpsest (*h*), a 6th cent. MS of the Apocalypse, Acts, and
Catholic Epistles.   M. Berger, its editor, has acutely pointed out
that, while the Acts and Apocalypse are Cyprianic in character,
the text of the Cath. Epp. is distinctly *late* African[2].   Indeed the
mere fact that the MS contains the Second Epistle of Peter is
enough to shew that it does not represent exclusively the old
African tradition.   But the mixed character of the text of *h* is
accounted for, when we recognise that while the late African
Church accepted S. Jerome's revision of the Gospels and enlarged
its Canon by receiving all seven Catholic Epistles, it nevertheless
retained the old version of the Acts and Apocalypse.

This remarkable eclecticism is also borne out by what we
actually find in some of S. Augustine's own works.   To begin
with we have his direct approval of S. Jerome's recension of the
Gospels.   In 403 AD, the year before the episode of Felix, S.
Augustine wrote to S. Jerome to express his doubts as to the
expediency of the great changes made by the latter in the Old
Testament but said at the same time : " Proinde non paruas Deo
gratias agimus de opere tuo quod *Euangelium* ex Graeco interpretatus es, quia paene in omnibus nulla offensio est."   Nor was this
approval academic only.   The evidence that the Gospel text in S.

---

[1] See Note 1 for the text of what S. Augustine read.
[2] S. Berger, *Le Palimpseste de Fleury,* p. 18.

Augustine's great critical work *de Consensu Euangelistarum* (circ.
400 AD) was based exclusively on the Vulgate is simply over-
whelming. The circumstance that the work includes several well-
known references to Old Latin readings (given as the text of
'some codices') has apparently obscured the fact that the text
accepted by S. Augustine as the base of his explanations is not a
form however late of the so-called *Vetus Itala*, but the Revised
Version of S. Jerome itself with all its peculiarities. A full examination of the Gospel text of the *de Consensu* is given in Note II to
this Essay; I shall here merely quote the judgment of Sabatier,
who will certainly not be accused of prejudice in such a case as
this. Speaking of sources whence quotations from the '*Itala*' may
be drawn, he says (*Praef. ad vol.* i, p. lvii): "Leve etiam modicum-
que est quod suppeditarunt libri *de consensu Evangelistarum*.
Collatis namque his Augustini libris cum Vulgata nostra, utraque
interpretatio una & eadem esse visa est; quod tamen de unis acci-
piendum est Evangeliis, quorum Augustinus interpretationem ab
Hieronymo adornatum sic adhibuit, ut nihilominus alios Scripturæ
libros, tam ipsius novi, quàm veteris Testamenti, juxta antiquam
LXX. interpretationem laudarit. Hinc quamvis nullas Evange-
liorum ex eo libro, plurimas tamen Actuum Apostolorum, necnon
& Epistolarum & Apocalypsis sententias à Vulgata nostra discre-
pantes reperimus, nec prætermisimus."

The mass of evidence which I have collected in the Note upon
the Biblical text of the *de Consensu* will I think carry conviction.
In the work, therefore, for which accuracy of textual detail was
most necessary S. Augustine used the Vulgate as the basis of his
argument. A recognition of this fact will clear up many difficulties
presented by the Gospel quotations in the rest of his later works.
Their general character is a Vulgate base with occasional Old
Latin readings. This non-Vulgate element is mostly late African,
and not so far as we know North Italian, in character; its insertion into the Vulgate text appears to be mostly fortuitous. That
is to say, he quotes a verse (e.g. in his Homilies on S. John) in
accordance sometimes with the Vulgate, sometimes with an Old
Latin reading, the latter being perhaps due to a reminiscence of
the text of his younger days. In other words he is just such an
authority as the 'mixed' MSS *ff*[1] or *l*, and only of independent value

for the criticism of the pre-Hieronymian texts where he differs
from the Vulgate.

'But', it will be said, 'is it not the case that S. Augustine used
a certain form of the Old Latin called by him *Itala interpretatio*,
which he praises as *uerborum tenacior*?'

This objection, which I think fairly expresses what is generally
held about S. Augustine's text, is based of course upon the famous
passage in the *De Doctrina Christiana* ii 22, where he says: "in
ipsis autem interpretationibus Itala ceteris praeferatur, nam est
uerborum tenacior cum perspicuitate sententiae". It is generally
assumed that *Itala* cannot refer to the Vulgate, because S. Augustine notoriously used the Old Latin, and held the LXX in very
high esteem. But that this difficulty was not felt in ancient times
is sufficiently proved by the quotation from S. Isidore's *Etymo-
logium* which stands as a motto to this Essay. I trust also that the
facts which I have brought forward about the *de Consensu* will help
to remove the difficulty, at least so far as regards the text of the
Gospels.

There are many objections to taking '*Itala*' to mean a certain
Old Latin text out of the many then extant, especially if it refers
to the forms of the New Testament. It has often been urged by
Bentley and others that S. Augustine never again praises this
hypothetical version, though he does elsewhere praise S. Jerome's
translation of the Prophets for its fidelity (*De Ciuit. Dei* xviii 42).
A more serious difficulty is that it is not usual for S. Augustine
when referring to the various forms of the Old Latin to call them
interpretationes. It is true that he speaks vaguely of *interpretum
numerositas* and uses similar phrases in speaking of what happened
in the first ages of the faith; but his usual way of speaking of
what we call Old Latin readings is that such and such a translation
is found 'in some codices'. Once at least he speaks of a reading
which is attested by S. Cyprian as found 'in many codices, but
they are African' (*codices plurimos uerumtamen afros*, Retr. i 21).
On the other hand S. Augustine actually uses *interpretari* of
S. Jerome's revision of the Gospels, as opposed to 'Old Latin' in
general, and the same is true to a still greater extent for the Old
Testament.

But the form of the sentence 'in ipsis *autem* interpretationibus' shews that the words must be taken with what goes before, and in the attempts to identify the *Itala* I do not think sufficient weight has hitherto been generally allowed to the nature of S. Augustine's argument in the five chapters preceding *De Doct. Christ.* ii 22, or to the examples he has used to support it.

He says in § 16: "propter diuersitates ut dictum est interpretum, illarum linguarum est cognitio necessaria. qui enim Scripturas ex hebraea lingua in graecam uerterunt numerari possunt, latini autem interpretes nullo modo; ut enim cuique primis fidei temporibus in manus uenit codex graecus et aliquantulum facultatis sibi utriusque linguae habere uidebatur, ausus est interpretari". After these celebrated words he goes on immediately to say that this state of things is not altogether unfortunate (§ 17): "Quae quidem res plus adiuuit intellegentiam quam impediuit, si modo legentes non sint neglegentes. nam nonnullas obscuriores sententias plurium codicum saepe manifestabit[1] inspectio." Here follow four instances, all of which are of the highest importance for understanding his point of view, both in respect of the examples themselves and of the way in which they are introduced. The first two are from Isaiah and contain a comparison, not of two Old Latin texts with each other, but of *the Old Latin* with *the modern Vulgate*. He says: "sicut illud Isaiae prophetae unus interpres ait *Et domesticos seminis tui ne despexeris; alius autem ait Et carnem tuam ne despexeris*". The first passage is Isaiah lviii 7 from the LXX, the second is the same passage from the Vulgate. A little lower down he goes on to say: "Item illud eiusdem Isaiae prophetae *Nisi credideritis non intellegetis* alius interpretatus est *Nisi credideritis non permanebitis*," i.e. a quotation of Isaiah vii 9, first from the LXX, then from the Vulgate. All this agrees with what he says in § 22 (quoted below): "As far as the O. T. is concerned the authority of the LXX is paramount; yet, as I said above, the collation of those translators who have stuck more closely (*tenacius*) to the words is not without its use." Evidently therefore this sentence refers to the pair of examples which I have just quoted, and with regard to which S. Augustine says that both translations are good for edification. One of these translations is the Latin rendering of the

---

[1] *Ed.* manifestavit.

LXX; hence the other, with which S. Augustine has 'collated' Isaiah vii 9 and lviii 7, is that translation which 'sticks more closely to the words'. But this alternative text is none other than the Vulgate!

To these examples from Isaiah are added one from the Psalms, a book for which S. Augustine in common with the rest of the Western Church never thought of using an *interpretatio* from the Hebrew[1], and one from the book of Wisdom, of which the Hebrew does not exist. In the latter case he blames the common reading (*spuria*) *uitulamina* in Wisd iv 3, and wishes to substitute *adulterinae plantationes*; but he says that the former reading— which by the way is attested by S. Optatus—is so common 'ut uix inueniatur aliter scriptum'. Here we seem to be dealing with a mere conjectural emendation from the Greek. In the example from the Psalms he says 'quidam codices habent *acuti pedes*' in Ps xiii 3 for *ueloces pedes*, and he rejects the former reading absolutely, saying that it is a mere mistranslation of the Greek ὀξύς. All extant Latin authorities have here *ueloces*, but it is probable that *acuti* is the genuine African rendering in this phrase. The verse is not quoted by S. Cyprian; but in Ps xliv 1 for ὀξυγράφου, where most Latins have *uelociter scribentis*, he has *acute scribentis* (*Test* II 29 codd. opt)[2]. This rough 'comparative criticism' of Latin variants by means of the Greek is doubtless what S. Augustine means by the words which sum up the discussion at the end of § 21: "plurimum hic quoque iuuat interpretum numerositas collatis codicibus inspecta atque discussa, tantum abest falsitas; nam codicibus emendandis primitus debet inuigilare solertia eorum qui Scripturas diuinas nosse desiderant, ut emendatis non emendati cedant, ex eo duntaxat interpretationis genere uenientes". He means, I suppose, that we may emend one Old Latin codex by another, or by the Greek itself, but we cannot correct a translation from the Hebrew by a translation from the Greek, or *vice versa*, for both of these are authoritative.

Both the Greek and the Hebrew are authoritative, and, as he endeavoured to shew by his examples from Isaiah, both are

---

[1] Cf. especially § 20 *ante med.*

[2] So the Oxford MS O₁; L has *acute scribens*: Hartel's text has the common reading.

spiritually instructive even where they differ. Yet there must come places where we have to choose between them, and he goes on to say (§ 22): " In ipsis autem interpretationibus Itala ceteris praeferatur ". Taken with what has gone before, does it not seem probable that the other *interpretatio,* which is not the LXX, is here meant? S. Augustine does not say he always uses the ' Itala'; indeed his whole argument is to prove that to the understanding man the very diversities of translations are instructive. But we have seen that he does sometimes use the Vulgate Gospels, especially where minute accuracy is required, while in the Old Testament we have seen that while habitually using the LXX—i.e. the Old Latin—he values the new translation highly and occasionally uses it for comparison[1].

I venture to think that S. Augustine, while writing *De Doct. Christ.* ii 22, had in mind the *Epistula ad Damasum,* S. Jerome's celebrated preface to the Vulgate Gospels. The same sequence of thought is expressed in both passages in the same order though in different language. For purposes of comparison I give the two passages in parallel columns.

Aug. *de Doct. Christ.* ii 22	Hieron. *Ep. ad Damasum*
In ipsis autem interpretationibus Itala ceteris praeferatur, nam est uerborum tenacior cum perspicuitate sententiae.	Si enim *Latinis* exemplaribus fides est adhibenda, respondeant quibus: tot sunt paene quot codices.
Et *Latinis* quibuslibet *emendandis* Graeci adhibeantur in quibus	Sin autem *ueritas est quaerenda* de pluribus, cur non *ad Graecam originem reuertentes* ea quae...aut addita sunt aut mutata *corrigimus?*

---

[1] E.g. *De Doct. Christ.* iv 16, where Am vi 1—6 is quoted expressly from the Vulgate. This latter part of the work dates from 426 AD. It is probable that in 397 AD, when the first three books up to iii 35 were written, S. Jerome's Pentateuch was not yet issued. Possibly some expressions may have been altered when the second edition, which we now possess, was published. The only quotation of any significance from the Gospels in this part of the work is in ii 62, where Mt xi 28—30 is cited with all the characteristics of S. Augustine's quotations from memory. They are :—(i) *Vulgate element,* reficiam uos; (ii) *African element,* sarcina; (iii) *Peculiar elements* (i.e. inaccuracies), (1) *om.* omnes, (2) lene *for* ' bonum ' (*afr.*) *or* ' suaue ' (*eur-rg*).

LXX interpretum
quod *ad uetus testamentum*
attinet
excellit auctoritas...sed tamen
ut superius dixi horum quoque
interpretum qui uerbis tenacius
inhaeserunt conlatio non est in-
utilis ad explanandum saepe sen-
tentiam. Latini ergo ut dicere
coeperam codices ueteris testamenti si necesse fuerit Graecorum
auctoritate emendandi sunt...

Libros autem *noui testamenti* si
quid in Latinis uarietatibus titubat
Graecis cedere oportere *non dubium
est*, et maxime qui apud Ecclesias
doctiores et diligentiores repperi-
untur.

Neque uero ego *de ueteri disputo
testamento* quod *a LXX senioribus*
in Graecam linguam
uersum tertio gradu ad nos
usque peruenit. Non quaero quid
Aquila quid Symmachus sapiant,
quare Theodotion inter nouos et
ueteres medius incedat: sit illa *uera
interpretatio quam apostoli pro-
bauerunt.*

De nouo nunc loquor *testamento*
quod *Graecum* esse
non dubium est.

The last clause of this extract (which has no parallel in the
Ep. ad Damasum) I believe to be a direct reference to the one
great Biblical scholar of the day, the learned and industrious
S. Jerome himself.

One objection remains to be noticed. If S. Augustine was
thinking of the Vulgate, why should he call it Italian? I do not
think this objection is fatal. In spite of all that has been written
on the word *italus* to prove that it meant in the fourth century
North Italian, few will doubt that it might mean Italian in a
more general sense in the work of an African writing to Africans[1].
At least Arnobius the African twice calls Latin *sermo italus*. Now
the Vulgate Gospels, the first part of the new work to come out,
were published in Italy at the instigation and under the patronage
of the Pope of Rome. And though S. Jerome had gone to
Bethlehem when the *Doctrina Christiana* was being written,
S. Augustine was not aware of the fact, as he sent about this
time letters to S. Jerome to Italy, where they were opened and
read by his enemies. As opposed to the 'African codices' or

---

[1] On this point see Rönsch, *Collectanea* 266, on the phrase of Nonius Marcellus:
'ita ut nunc Itali dicunt'.

the Greek Bible the Vulgate was 'Italian' to S. Augustine[1]. But this does not directly affect the main point which I have endeavoured to prove; which is, that the evidence afforded by the Gospel text of the *De Consensu* on the one hand, and the arguments and examples used by S. Augustine in *De Doctrina Christiana* ii 17—21 on the other, so decisively point to the conclusion that the translation which he calls *Itala* is the Revised Version of S. Jerome, that very strong positive evidence would be required to make any other identification equally probable.

---

[1] For S. Augustine's use of the word *italus* elsewhere we may compare *de Ordine* ii 45. Speaking of a correct style and pronunciation he says: "me enim ipsum, cui magna necessitas fuit ista perdiscere, adhuc in multis uerborum sonis *Itali* exagitant, et a me uicissim quod ad ipsum sonum adtinet reprehenduntur. aliud est enim esse arte aliud gente securum....... Barbarismorum autem genus nostris temporibus tale compertum est, ut et ipsa eius oratio barbara uideatur qua *Roma* seruata est." Here therefore the 'Italian' pronunciation is that of Rome itself, a pronunciation which the African S. Augustine, in spite of a good education, had only imperfectly attained.

NOTE I.

S. Augustine and Felix the Manichee.

The following extract is taken from Aug. *contra Felicem*, i.e. the report of the trial of Felix (C. S. E. L. xxv. pp. 802—807, edited by Zycha). In the footnotes to the quotation of Lc xxiv 36—49 I have given the readings of Wordsworth and White's text of the Vulgate (= *vg*), in the few places where it differs from the *contra Felicem*.

AUGUSTINUS *dixit*: Quoniam ergo tu[1] probare non potuisti quomodo sit Manichaeus apostolus Christi, et exigis ut ego probem quomodo miserit Spiritum Sanctum Paracletum quem promisit, ut tunc respuas scripturas Manichaei, si inueneris inpletam promissionem Christi praeter scripturas Manichaei, quamuis prior ad interrogata mea respondere debueris, tamen ecce ego prior respondeo et ostendo tibi, quando missus sit Spiritus Sanctus quem Christus promisit. *et accedit ad Euangelium et Actus Apostolorum.*

Et cum accepisset codicem Euangelii, recitauit: [36]Dum autem haec loquuntur, stetit Iesus in medio eorum et dixit eis: pax uobis; ego sum, nolite timere. *et cum legeret, dixit:* hoc post resurrectionem. *et cum dixisset, legit:* [37]conturbati uero et conterriti aestimabant se spiritum uidere. [38]et dixit eis: quid turbati estis et cogitationes ascendunt in corda uestra? [39]uidete manus meas et pedes, quia ego ipse sum; palpate et uidete, quia spiritus carnem et ossa non habet, sicut me uidetis habere. [40]et cum hoc dixisset, ostendit eis manus et pedes. [41]Adhuc autem illis non credentibus et mirantibus prae gaudio dixit: habetis hic aliquid quod manducetur? [42]at illi obtulerunt ei

36 haec autem *vg*   Iesus stetit *vg*   dixit] dicit *vg*   37 existimabant *vg*   39 ipse ego *vg*

[1] I.e. Felix.

partem piscis assi et fauum mellis. ⁴³et cum manducasset coram eis,
sumens reliquias dedit eis. ⁴⁴Et dixit ad eos : haec sunt uerba quae
locutus sum ad uos cum adhuc essem uobiscum, quoniam necesse est
inpleri omnia quae scripta sunt in lege Moysi et prophetis et psalmis
de me. ⁴⁵tunc aperuit illis sensum ut intellegerent scripturas, ⁴⁶et
dixit eis : quoniam sic scriptum est et sic oportebat Christum pati et
resurgere a mortuis die tertio, ⁴⁷et praedicari in nomine eius paenitentiam et remissionem peccatorum in omnes gentes, incipientibus ab
Hierusalem. ⁴⁸uos autem estis testes horum. ⁴⁹et ego mittam promissum patris mei in uos ; uos autem sedete in ciuitate, quoad usque
induamini uirtutem ex alto. *et cum reddidisset codicem Euangelii,
accipit Actus Apostolorum......*

Et recitauit ex Actibus Apostolorum¹: ¹Primum quidem sermonem Ac i
feci de omnibus, o Theophile, quae coepit Iesus facere et docere ²in die 1—26
quo apostolos elegit per Spiritum Sanctum et praecepit praedicare
Euangelium : ³quibus praebuit se uiuum post passionem in multis
argumentis dierum uisus eis dies quadraginta et docens de regno Dei,
⁴et quomodo conuersatus est cum illis, et praecepit eis ne discederent ab
Hierosolymis, sed sustinerent pollicitationem Patris, quam audistis,
inquit, ex ore meo ; ⁵quoniam Iohannes quidem baptizauit aqua, uos
autem Spiritu Sancto incipietis baptizari, quem et accepturi estis non
post multos istos dies usque ad Pentecosten. ⁶illi ergo conuenientes
interrogabant eum dicentes : Domine, si in hoc tempore praesentabis
regnum Israhel? ⁷ille autem dixit : nemo potest cognoscere tempus
quod pater posuit in sua potestate ; ⁸sed accipietis uirtutem Spiritus
Sancti superuenientem in uos, et eritis mihi testes apud Hierosolymam
et in tota Iudaea et Samaria et usque in totam terram. ⁹cum haec
diceret, nubes suscepit eum et sublatus est ab eis. ¹⁰et quomodo
contemplantes erant cum iret in caelum, ecce duo uiri astabant illis in
ueste alba, ¹¹qui dixerunt ad eos : uiri Galilaei, quid statis respicientes

---

44 Mosi *vg. codd. opt*   46 die tertia *vg (exc* AY)   47 Hierosolyma *vg*
49 mitto *vg. codd. opt*

1 fecimus *Fund. cod. opt*   2 die qua *Fund*; usque in diem quo *de Cons*   prae-
ceperit *Fund*   et praecepit] mandans iussit *de Cons*   3 uisus est eis per *Fund*
4 et 1°] *om. Fund. codd*   est] sit *Fund*   5 dies istos *Fund*   6 ergo] quidem *Fund*
conuenientes] cum uenissent *Fund*   hoc in tempore *Fund*   praesentabis] repre-
sentaberis et quando *Fund*   8 Hierusalem *Fund*   terram] ¶ *Fund*

¹ The variants given are those of Aug's quotations of Ac i, ii in *contra Ep.
Fundamenti* (C. S. E. L. xxv, pp. 203, 204). For the first two verses of Acts there
is a further parallel in Aug. *de Consensu* iv 8, a quotation made probably from
memory. The Vulgate text of Ac i 1—4 is given below, p. 70.

in caelum? iste Iesus qui adsumptus est in caelum a uobis sic ueniet, quemadmodum uidistis eum euntem in caelum. [12] tunc reuersi sunt Hierosolymam a monte qui uocatur Eleon, qui est iuxta Hierosolymam sabbati habens iter. [13] et cum introissent, ascenderunt in superiora, ubi habitabant Petrus et Iohannes, Iacobus et Andreas, Philippus et Thomas, Bartholomaeus et Matthaeus, Iacobus Alphaei et Symon Zelotes et Iudas Iacobi. [14] et erant perseuerantes omnes unanimes in orationibus cum mulieribus et Maria quae fuerat mater Iesu et fratribus eius. [15] et in diebus illis exurrexit Petrus in medio discentium, et dixit —fuit autem turba in uno hominum quasi cxx :—[16] uiri fratres, oportet adinpleri scripturam istam, quam praedixit Spiritus Sanctus ore sancti Dauid de Iuda, qui fuit deductor illorum qui comprehenderunt Iesum, [17] quoniam adnumeratus erat inter nos, qui habuit sortem huius ministerii. [18] hic igitur possedit agrum de mercede iniustitiae suae, et collum sibi alligauit et deiectus in faciem diruptus est medius et effusa sunt omnia uiscera eius. [19] quod et cognitum factum est omnibus qui inhabitabant Hierosolymam, ita ut uocaretur ager ille ipsorum lingua Acheldemach, id est ager sanguinis. [20] scriptum est enim in libro Psalmorum : Fiat uilla eius deserta, et non sit qui inhabitet in ea, et episcopatum eius accipiat alter. [21] oportet itaque ex his uiris qui conuenerunt nobiscum in omni tempore quo introiuit super nos et excessit Dominus Iesus Christus, [22] incipiens a baptismo Iohannis usque in illum diem quo adsumptus est a nobis, testem resurrectionis eius nobiscum esse. [23] et statuit duos, Ioseph qui uocabatur Barsabas qui et Iustus, et Matthiam. [24] et precatus dixit : Tu Domine cordis omnium intellector, ostende ex his duobus quem elegisti [25] ad suscipiendum locum huius ministerii et adnuntiationis, a qua excessit Iudas ambulare in locum suum. [26] et dederunt sortes suas, et cecidit sors super Matthiam, et simul deputatus est cum undecim apostolis duodecimus. *et cum legisset, dixit:* Audiuimus quis ordinatus est in locum Iudae traditoris... *Et cum dixisset, legit:* [1] In illo tempore quo subpletus est dies Pentecostes fuerunt omnes simul in uno. [2] et factus est subito de caelo sonus, quasi ferretur flatus uehemens, et inpleuit totam illam domum in qua erant sedentes. [3] et uisae sunt illis linguae diuisae quasi ignis, qui et insedit super unumquemque eorum. [4] et inpleti sunt omnes Spiritu Sancto, et

---

15 discentium] dicentium *codd. omn,* audientium *Zycha* ! (*cf* Cypr 738) cxx:—[16] uiri fratres] centum uiginti uiri—fratres *Zycha*

1 In illo tempore] § *Fund* illo] loco *Fel. codd. omn* (legit in loco: tempore, quo *Zycha*) simul in uno] eadem animatione simul in unum *Fund* 2 totum illum locum *Fund* quo *Fund*

coeperunt loqui uariis linguis quomodo Spiritus dabat eis pronuntiare.
[5]Hierosolymis autem fuerunt habitatores Iudaei, homines ex omni
natione quae est sub caelo. [6]et cum facta esset uox, collecta est turba
et confusa, quoniam audiebat unusquisque suo sermone et suis linguis
loquentes eos. [7]stupebant autem et admirabantur ad inuicem dicentes :
Nonne omnes qui loquuntur natione sunt Galilaei ? [8]et quomodo
agnoscimus in illis sermonem in quo nati sumus ? [9]Parthi Medi et
Elamitae, et qui inhabitant Mesopotamiam Iudaeam et Cappadociam,
Pontum Asiam [10]Frigiam et Pamphyliam, Aegyptum et partes Libyae
quae est ad Cyrenem, et qui aderant Romani [11]Iudaeique et proselyti,
Cretenses et Arabes, audiebant loquentes illos suis linguis magualia
Dei. *et cum recitaret, dixit :* Audisti nunc iam Spiritum Sanctum et
quomodo sit missus ? quod de me exegisti probaui.....

4 uariis] *om. Fund*   5 habitantes *Fund*   6 confusa]+est *Fund*
9 Parthi]+et *Fel. codd (non opt)*   Medi et] *om.* et *Fund*   Iudaeam] Armeniam
Fund   10 Frygiam *Fund*; Phrigiamque *Fel. cod*, Phrygiam *Fel. cod Zycha*
partes Libyae] regiones Africae *Fund*   aduenerant *Fund*   11 Iudaeique et
proselyti] et Iudaei incolae et *Fund*   Dei]+[12]stupebant autem et haesitabant
ob id quod factum est dicentes quidnam hoc uult esse? [13]alii autem inridebant
dicentes : Hi musto omnes onerati sunt *Fund*

The close agreement of the text of Lc xxiv in this extract
with the Vulgate, and of Ac i and ii with that of the book
contra Ep. Fundamenti is obvious at a mere glance. Moreover
the strongly 'African' character of the text of the Acts will be
at once visible to anyone at all familiar with the Cod. Bobiensis (*k*)
or the Fleury Palimpsest (*h*). I need only mention *contemplari*
(Mc x 27 *k*, Ac iii 3, 5 *h*), *Eleon* (Mc xi 1, xiii 3, xiv 26 *k*),
discens (Mt viii 21 etc *k*, Ac vi 5, ix 10 *h*), and the repeated use
of *quomodo* for ὥς ; these with many other points of language are
hardly found except in African documents[1].

For the sake of comparison I repeat the first four verses of the
Acts as read in *contra Felicem*, arranged parallel with the Vulgate.
Sixteen variations will be found in four verses, some of them of the
most serious kind (such as the complete omission of *adsumtus est*
in Aug ³/₃). On the other hand in the fourteen verses of the quotation from S. Luke the text of the *contra Felicem* only differs nine
times from the Vulgate, all nine being minor points.

[1] For a more extended discussion see P. Corssen, *Der Cyprianische Text der
Acta Apostolorum*, Berlin, 1892.

Aug	Vulgate
contra Fel. (cf. *contr. ep. Fund*)	from cod. Amiatinus

Primum quidem sermonem	Primum quidem sermonem
feci de omnibus, o Theophile,	feci de omnibus, o Theophile,
quae coepit Iesus facere et docere	quae coepit Iesus facere et docere
²in die quo apostolos elegit	²*usque* in diem qua praecipi*ens* apostol*is*
per Spiritum Sanctum ∧	per Spiritum Sanctum
et praecep*it praedicare*	*quos* elegit
Euangelium :	*adsumtus est* ∧
³quibus praebuit se uiuum	³quibus *et* praebuit se *ipsum* uiuum
post passionem ∧	post passionem *suam*
in multis argumentis *dierum*	in multis argumentis
uisus eis ∧ dies XL	*per* dies XL *apparens* eis
et *docens* de regno Dei,	et *loquens* de regno Dei
⁴et *quomodo conuersatus est cum illis,*	⁴et *conuescens*
et praecepit eis	praecepit eis
ne discederent ab Hierosolymis,	ab Hierosolymis ne discederent
sed *sustinerent*	sed *expectarent*
pollicitationem Patris	*promissionem* Patris
quam audistis inquit *ex ore meo*	quam audistis [inquit] *per os meum*

I do not see any reason to doubt the accuracy of the account of the trial of Felix. In many parts the work reads like the transcript of a shorthand report, e.g. *contra Fel* ii 14 (*Zycha*, p. 843),

> AUG. dixit: Anathemandus est error, qui dicit corruptibilem Deum, an non est anathemandus ?
> FEL. dixit: Iterum dic.
> AUG. dixit: Anathemandus est error, qui dicit corruptibilem Deum, an non est anathemandus ?

And again, a little lower down,

> FEL. dixit: Non intellexi, quod dixisti.

Unless this is mere literary fraud, the text of *contra Felicem* must rest on mechanical reporting; if so, the probability is all the stronger that the words of the Biblical text of Lc xxiv, and of Ac i and ii, were taken down as they were read out of the codices.

This agrees too with what S. Augustine himself says of the book in *Retr* ii 8: "Gesta sunt ecclesiastica, sed inter meos libros computantur." The MS tradition of the work appears to be fairly good, though all known copies are somewhat late and belong to a single family. Zycha's oldest MS is of the 12th century. In Ac i 15, where all Zycha's MSS have *dicentium* for *discentium*, the MS of *contra Felicem* in the Cambridge University Library (Ii. III. 2) has the further corruption *docentium*. The parallel quotation in *contra Ep. Fundamenti* rests upon much more ancient MS authority, and contains on the whole more primitive readings. This is especially the case from Ac ii 9 onwards.

The extract I have given from the *contra Felicem* is thus doubly valuable to the textual critic. On the one hand it affords one of the clearest proofs of S. Augustine's use of the Vulgate Gospels at the beginning of the fifth century, and on the other it gives us a continuous text of the Old African version of the greater part of the first two chapters of the Acts, a section altogether wanting in the Fleury MS, the first fragment of which begins at Ac iii 2. A quotation so long and so curious as that of Ac i and ii in the *contra Felicem* has not of course remained unnoticed, the most satisfactory investigation of it being Corssen's tract *Der Cyprianische Text der Acta Apostolorum* noticed above. Corssen rightly brings out its thoroughly Cyprianic character, and notices that the quotation from S. Luke which precedes it "comes quite close to the Vulgate" (p. 25), but he only uses this circumstance to disprove Ziegler's assertion that S. Augustine always quotes from a single form of text. He does not apparently notice that S. Augustine, in changing from the Vulgate Gospels to what strikes us as an ancient 'African' text of the Acts, is still consistent with himself. With Ziegler I recognise that S. Augustine, like S. Cyprian, habitually used a single text, at least from about 400 AD onwards; but this text, unlike S. Cyprian's, is of a different character in different books of the New Testament.

NOTE II.

The Gospel text in Aug. de Consensu Euangelistarum.

Notwithstanding Sabatier's explicit judgment, quoted above on p. 59, the proofs in this Note that the Gospel text in the *de Consensu* was taken by S. Augustine himself from the Vulgate may not be altogether superfluous. I have used the following additional abbreviations:

vg = Wordsworth and White's text of the Vulgate,
vg. *cl* = the Clementine text of the Vulgate,
Aug. *cons* = text of *De Consensu Euangelistarum.*

Single MSS of the Vulgate are cited by Wordsworth and White's notation.

The references to Aug. *cons* are by the smaller chapters of the Paris reprint of the Benedictine edition (1836—1839).

1. *The quotations have not been assimilated wholesale to the Vulgate in the MS transmission of Aug.* cons.

This appears from e.g. Aug. *cons* i 44 (= Esai ii 5—21); i 47 (= Esai lii 13—liv 5); iv 9 (= Ac i 1, 2); iii 84 (= Ac x 41); iii 70 (= 1 Cor xv 3—8). In all these passages the text differs greatly from the Vulgate.

2. *The Gospel quotations in Aug.* cons *as they stand, both long and short, agree so closely with the Vulgate as to render it certain that they were derived from it.*

α. The actual amount of difference between Aug. *cons* and the text of Wordsworth and White hardly comes up to *one varia-*

tion in three verses, the most trifling variations (except spelling) being included.

An example, chosen at random, exhibiting the mutual relations of Aug. *cons*, the Vulgate and *f* will make this clear. As hitherto the text of *f* has been supposed to represent the basis not only of the Vulgate but also of Aug, I give it in full with variants of vg and Aug (*cons* iii 46) below.

Joh xix 4—16 *from cod. Brixianus* (*f*)

(*Italics* mark the readings where *vg* and *Aug* agree against *f*).

[4]*exiuit* iterum pilatus foras. et *dixit* eis. ecce adduco uobis cum foras. ut *sciatis* quia *non inuenio ullam* causam *in eo*. [5]exiit ergo iesus *foras*. *habens* spineam coronam et *tunicam purpuream*. et *dixit* eis. ecce homo. [6]cum ergo uidissent eum *principes sacerdotum* et ministri *eorum*. *exclamauerunt* dicentes. crucifige crucifige *eum*. dicit eis pilatus accipite eum uos. et crucifigite ego enim. non inuenio in eo causam. [7]responderun*t* iudaei. nos legem habemus. et secundum legem. debet mori. quia filium dei se fecit. [8]cum ergo audisset pilatus *hoc uerbum*. magis timuit. [9]et *introiuit iterum in praetorio*. et *ait* ad iesum. unde es tu. iesus autem responsum non dedit ei. [10]dicit ergo ei pilatus. mihi non loqueris. nescis quia potestatem habeo crucifigere **te**. et potestatem habeo dimittere te. [11]respondit iesus. non haberes *in me ullam potestatem*. nisi tibi data *fuisset* desuper. propterea. qui *me tibi tradidit*. maius peccatum habet. [12]*et* exinde quaerebat pilatus dimittere eum. iudaei autem clamabant dicentes si hunc *dimiseris*. non es amicus caesaris. omnis *enim* qui se regem facit. contradicit caesari. [13]pilatus *autem his uerbis auditis*. adduxit foras iesum. et sedit pro tribunali in locum qui dicitur litho-

Variants of vg *and* Aug. **4** exiit *vg Aug*   dicit *vg Aug*   eum uobis *Aug* cognoscatis *vg Aug*   in eo nullam causam inuenio *vg Aug*   **5** foras] *om. vg Aug* habens] portans *vg Aug*   tun. pur.] purpureum uestimentum *vg Aug*   dicit *vg Aug*   **6** pr. sac.] pontifices *vg Aug*   eorum] *om. vg Aug*   clamabant *vg Aug*   eum] *om.* vg (*sic*) *Aug*   **7** resp.]+ei *vg Aug*   **8** hunc sermonem *vg Aug*   **9** ingressus est praetorium iterum *vg Aug*   ait] dicit *vg Aug* **11** in me u. pot.] pot. aduersum me ullam *vg Aug* (aduersus *Aug*ᵒᵈ)   data fuisset] esset datum *vg*, datum esset *Aug*   tradidit me tibi *vg Aug*   **12** et] *om. vg Aug* pilatus quaerebat *Aug*   dimittis *vg Aug*   enim] *om. vg Aug*   **13** autem] ergo *vg Aug*   cum audisset hos sermones *vg Aug*   in loco *Aug*ᵉᵈ   lithostrotos *Aug*ᵒᵈ, lithostrotus *vg* (*sic*)

stratus. hebraice autem *gennesar.* ¹⁴erat autem parasceue paschae.
hora quasi sexta. et *dixit* iudaeis. ecce rex uester. ¹⁵illi autem
exclamauerunt. tolle. tolle. crucifige eum. dixit eis pilatus. regem
uestrum crucifigam. responderunt *principes sacerdotum.* non habemus
regem nisi caesarem. ¹⁶tunc ergo. tradidit eis illum. ut cruci-
figeretur.

13 gabbatha *vg Aug*   14 dicit *vg Aug* (dicit ergo *Aug,* *taking up the Gospel*
narrative after some remarks)   15 clamabant *vg Aug*   pr. sac.] pontifices
vg Aug

Here then in 13 verses Augustine goes with the best text of
the Vulgate against *f* 26 times, against both *f* and vg three (or
four) times, with *f* against vg not at all! And no known purely
Old Latin MS is so near to vg as *f.*

β. The coincidences of Aug. *cons* with vg include many
readings and renderings found in no Old Latin authority—
readings therefore which probably originated with S. Jerome.
Examples are :—

Aug. *cons* ii 17 *sciscitabatur* = Mt ii 4 vg (= ἐπυνθάνετο); but
quaes[iu]it, requisiuit, interrogabat lat. vt
Aug. *cons* ii 138 *in sermone meo* = Joh viii 31 vg; but *in uerbo meo*
lat. vt, incl Aug. *Joh* 41
Aug. *cons* ii 70 *eiciat* = Mt ix 38 vg. *codd. opt* (= ἐκβάλῃ); but *mittat*
lat. vt-vg.*cl*

The last is an especially noteworthy case, as any text to
which the MSS of Aug. *cons* would be likely to be conformed in
later times would almost certainly have *mittat.*

γ. The differences between Aug. *cons* and the text of
Wordsworth and White are mostly minutiae, and in these cases
Aug. *cons* generally has support from some MSS of the Vulgate,
i.e. *the variations do not go beyond the variations actually found*
in MSS of the Vulgate itself.
Examples :—

Aug. *cons* iii 27 (Joh xviii 28) *ad Caipham* for *a Caiapha.* Our
knowledge of the text of Aug. *cons* is not exact enough to determine
the spelling of the proper name, but *ad* for *a* is expressly attested by
the MSS and is required by the context. Among MSS of the Vulgate *ad*

Caipham (*Caiapha, Caifan,* etc) is read by Wordsworth's MI𝔅 CT ΘH SOXZ* BM𝔗 DE K W as well as *e a c ff f aur gat.*

Aug. *cons* iii 28 (Mt xxvii 9) *filii Israel* for *a filiis Isr.* filii israhel (or *filii srael* etc, as *f*) is also read by C(T) 𝔓^{mg}DLQ(R*) as well as G *f.*

Aug. *cons* ii 45 *codd* (Lc vi 17) *maritima tyri* for *maritima et tyri* ; 'maritima tyri' is read by H*ΘP and *a c e f ff q r* (hiat *b*), 'maritimaetyri' is read by MG.

3. *The few serious variations of Aug.* cons *from the Vulgate are very seldom Old Latin readings.*

In Aug. *cons* ii 71 there is a short quotation of Joh v 29 from the O. L., while in iv 6 Mt xxv 45 is cited from memory with the unsupported variant *quando* for *quamdiu,* and in iii 86 and iv 20 in the peroration of the books we have Joh xiv 21 with the O. L. *ostendam* for *manifestabo.* But these stand almost alone, unless we add the variations of Ac i 1, 2 in Aug. *cons* iv 9, which seems to be a quotation from memory of the African text as found e.g. in *contr. Fel* 804. Again, the readings *regnum euangelii* for *euangelii regnum* (Aug. *cons* ii 70 = Mt ix 35) and *gloria sua* for *gloria patris sui* (Aug. *cons* ii 111 = Mc viii 38) are absolutely unsupported by any known authority, and are most probably due to S. Augustine himself. That he was now and then capable of a simple slip is shewn by his substitution of Barnabas for Silas in an allusion to Ac xvi 25 (Aug. *Joh* 113).

There are two passages where S. Augustine expressly quotes a Gospel by name for a reading which it is hard to believe was anything more than a mere blunder in the MS before him. These two passages in fact form the only argument for supposing that the text S. Augustine took as the basis for the *De consensu* was originally different from that of the Vulgate.

In Aug. *cons* ii 26 we read :—" *ille uero baptizabit uos Spiritu* " *Sancto.* De baptismo autem hoc [Ev. *sc.* Marci] ab utroque "[distat], quia non dixit *et igni* sed tantum *in Spiritu Sancto.* " Sicut enim Mt ita et Lc dixit et eodem ordine *Ipse uos baptizabit* " *in Spiritu et igni,* nisi quod Lc non addidit *Sancto,* sicut Mt dixit " *in Spiritu Sancto et igni.*" All these quotations agree literally with the Vulgate except for the omission of *Sancto* in Lc iii 16, a

reading for which there is some faint Greek evidence, but the only
Latin evidence which is quoted for it is a doubtful allusion in Tert.
de Bapt § 10. Is it not a simpler hypothesis to suppose that the
word was accidentally omitted in S. Augustine's codex? We know
at least from *Retr* ii 12 that S. Augustine in *Quaest. Ev* i 27 had
been deluded into unnecessary subtleties by the error of the codex
he was then using, which read *duobus* instead of *duodecim* in
Mt xx 17[1]. It is worth adding, lest it should be thought that S.
Augustine's express mention of readings usually shew variation
from the Vulgate, that in this very passage (Aug. *cons* ii 26) he
expressly says that *procumbens* is found in Mc i 7 and that *in
poenitentiam* is not added in Lc iii 16. This is true of the text of
Wordsworth and White in each place, but the exact contrary is the
case in every extant Old Latin text except *f*, which however differs
verbally in some other respects in both passages. Thus but for the
single omission of *Sancto* in Lc iii 16 Aug is here using a text
distinctively Vulgate in character.

Again in Aug. *cons* iii 25 we read: " Iam uero illud quod Mt ipsi
" Petro dictum fuisse asserit *Vere et tu ex illis eo, nam et loquela tua*
"*manifestum te faciet* (Mt xxvi 73); sicut Ioh eidem Petro dictum
"asseuerat " *Nonne ego te uidi in horto cum illo?* (Joh xviii 26);
" Mc autem inter se illos de Petro locutos dicit *Vere ex illis est,*
"*nam et Galilaeus est* (cf Mc xiv 70); sicut et Lc non Petro sed
" de Petro dicit *Alius quidam affirmabat dicens, Vere et hic cum
"*illo erat, nam et Galilaeus est* (Lc xxii 59)...". The true text of
Mc xiv 70 as witnessed by every other authority Greek and Latin,
including Aug himself at the beginning of the section, has *Petro* for
de Petro and *es* for *est* in each place, thereby rendering the remark
quoted above inaccurate. Aug seems in fact to confuse this remark
with that in the previous verse (Mc xiv 69), where the maid says
of Peter *Hic ex illis est*. Those who have occasion to work at
the diction of the parallel narratives of the Synoptists will not
wonder at occasional confusions of this kind in the most careful
writer.

I have treated these two passages more fully, because they are

---

[1] The present writer has in his possession a Vulgate Bible of the 14th cent.
which actually agrees with Aug in omitting s͞c͞o here; the ᴍꜱ has elsewhere several
readings of an interesting type, but this is no doubt a mere blunder.

I believe the only places where even a *prima facie* case can be raised against the hypothesis, that S. Augustine in the *De consensu* was working on a MS of the Vulgate[1].

The references to Various Readings in the De Consensu.

In several places S. Augustine gives various readings found in 'some codices'. This is his usual way of indicating an Old Latin reading as distinct from the Vulgate.

Aug. *cons* ii 31 nonnulli codices habent sec. Lucam (iii 22)...*Filius meus es tu, ego hodie genui te* ; quamquam in antiquioribus codicibus graecis non inueniri perhibeatur.

Aug. *cons* ii 70 In nominibus...discipulorum Lucas...a Mt (x 3) non discrepat, nisi in nomine Iudae Iacobi quem Mt 'Thaddaeum' appellat; nonnulli autem codices habent 'Lebdaeum'.[2]

Aug. *cons* ii 106 'Dalmanutha', quod in quibusdam codicibus legitur (Mc viii 10), non dixit Mt, sed 'Magedan'...Nam plerique codices non habent etiam sec. Mc nisi 'Magedan'.

(Aug. *cons* ii 128 codices ecclesiastici interpretationis : i.e. of Zech ix 9 LXX.)

Aug. *cons* iii 29 Si quis autem moueter quod hoc testimonium non inuenitur in Scriptura Hieremiae prophetae...primo nouerit quod non omnes codices Euangeliorum habere quod per Hieremiam dictum sit... sed tantum *per prophetam dicentem*... Sed utatur ista defensione cui placet ; mihi autem cur non placet haec causa est, quia et plures codices habent Hieremiae nomen, et qui diligentius in graecis exemplaribus Euangelium considerauerunt in antiquioribus graecis ita se perhibent inuenisse.......cur autem de nonnullis codicibus tolleretur, etc.

---

[1] Numerical results of a collation of Aug. *cons* (C) and Wordsworth's Vulgate (W) with cod. Brixianus (*f*) and with cod. Monacensis (*q*) in Mt i, ii (including stray quotations up to Aug. *cons* ii 13) and Mt xxvi 1—26 [63 verses in all]:

CW/*f*	68	CW/*q*	79
C*f*/W	9	C*q*/W	7
C/*f*W	11	C/*q*W	12
C/*f*/W	2	C/*q*/W	3
	90		101

[2] Cf. the early correction *iebdaeus* Mt x 3 *k*, where the first hand had written *iebbaeus*. The Benedictine editors of Aug read *Lebbaeum* with (? some) MSS.

The ꜱꜱ authorities for the four readings are as follows :

  ii 31 nonnulli codd. = D*d* *a b c ff* l r* Tyc Faust (*not contradicted by*
      Aug. *contra Faust*) Hil³ Iuv [not *e*, *f q* vg]

  ii 70 nonnulli codd. = D*d* *k* ['*Iud. Zelotes*' *a b h q gat* GE; *f* = ꙅᴿ;
      '*Thaddaeus*' vg]

  ii 106 quibusdam codd. = *f q* vg and Aug
      plerique codd. = D*d* *k* *a b c ff i r*

  iii 29 non omnes codd. *and* nonnullis codd. = *a b* [not *d* vg; *k* and *e* are
      not extant here]

NOTE.

If, as I have attempted to shew, S. Augustine accepted the Vulgate
for his text of the Gospels, the whole of the N.T. as used by him is
now represented in extant ꜱꜱ. It has long been recognised that the
Freising fragments, published by Ziegler and usually called *r*, give
S. Augustine's text of the Pauline Epistles; his text in the Apocalypse,
Acts, and Catholic Epistles is given by the Fleury Palimpsest, while in
the Apocalypse we have the additional evidence of Primasius. Hitherto
it has appeared surprising that none of our numerous Old Latin Codices
of the Gospels should correspond to S. Augustine's 'Itala', seeing that
the Augustinian text was so fully represented in our scanty list of Old
Latin authorities for the rest of the N.T. But now the matter is clear
enough. No 'Old Latin' ꜱꜱ could give the Augustinian text of the
Gospels, because the Augustinian text of the Gospels is the Vulgate.

APPENDIX.

THE S. GALLEN FRAGMENT OF JEREMIAH.

THE S. GALLEN FRAGMENT OF JEREMIAH.

Cod. Sangallensis No. 912 is a palimpsest, the upper writing being a Latin Glossary of the 9th cent. Nearly all the leaves have older writing underneath, very faint and brown, and quite illegible except where the pages have been stained with a blue reagent. Pp. 303, 304, 309, 310, 25, 26, 31, 32 (and no others) are taken from an Old Latin MS of Jeremiah, making two nearly complete pages of the older writing. This, which will be cited here as g, appears to date from the fifth century at least[1]. There are no signatures preserved, so that no idea can be formed of the original contents of the book. There are fifteen lines in a column, and only one column in a page, making the original page nearly a square of about 8 in.—that is, about the shape and size of the Bobbio Gospels (k). The bodkin lines are $3\frac{15}{16}$ in. apart for the columns, $\frac{3}{8}$ in. for the lines. The length of the lines varies from $3\frac{3}{4}$ to $4\frac{1}{4}$ in., mostly however they just reach 4 inches; the letters are $\frac{3}{16}$ in. high. The writing very much resembles the Old Latin fragments of the Gospels from the same Library, usually cited as n (in *Cod. Sangall.* 1394, tom. I), but the rather peculiar 'a' found in n does not occur.

The fragments of Jeremiah were edited by Tischendorf in the second edition (1861) of *Monumenta Sacra et Profana*. The MS, as Tischendorf says, is hard to read; but by the aid of a magnifying glass and a good light I have been able to read some words hitherto undeciphered. The mutilated fragments of Hier xvii are less clear than those of Hier xxix (49): I doubt if they would come out better in a photograph. It will be seen that in Hier xvii a third of each line has been altogether cut away.

---

[1] The regular use of 'd$\overline{\text{ms}}$' and 'd$\overline{\text{me}}$' (not 'd$\overline{\text{ns}}$' and 'd$\overline{\text{ne}}$') makes in favour of this early date.

Cod. S.
Gall 912
p. 25

CUIQUESECUNDUMUIASEIUS

ETSECUNDUMFRUCTUMCO

CITATIONUMEORUMRED

deREEIS·CLAMAUITPERDIX

₅ CONCREGAUITQUOSNONPE

PERIT·MULTOSPARIATSIBI

FILIOSAdquIRENSdIUITIAS

SUASNONCUMIUDICIOIN

p. 32

dIMIDIODIERUMEIUSdERE

₁₀ LINQUENTEUMETUSq·INNO

UISSIMOSUOERITSTULTUS·

THRONUSAUTEMUIRTUTIS·

EXALTATUSEST·ETENIMSANC

TIFICATIONOSTRAPATIENTIA

₁₅ ILLIUSISTRAEL·

(*fol.* 1 r)

---

2 Littera 'f' in *fructum* non liquet: habet Tisch.   3 'eorum red' et
5 'quos non pe': non legit Tisch.   6 'pariat': *rapiat* Tisch.   7 'a'
in *adquirens* legit Tisch., sed non exstat in membranis.   10 'm' in *eum* et
11 's' *ad fin.* non liquent: habet Tisch.   12 'r' et 's' in *uirtutis* non
liquent: *virtute* Tisch.   13 'etenim sanc': *et erit* — — Tisch.   14 'tie
in *patientia*, et partes 'n' et 't' 2ᵘ, non satis liquent: habet Tisch.

dmeomnesquite deʀelin
queʀuntconfundantuʀ
quidiscesseʀuntateʀʀa
scʀibantuʀinlibʀomoʀtis
5 quiadeʀelinqueʀ untfon
temuitaedṁi.cuʀamedme
etsaluuseʀo.tuesenimcla
ʀitasmea.eccehii.dicunt
mihiubiestueʀb umdṁi
10 ueniecoautem nonlabo
ʀauisubsequens teetdiē
hominisnonde sideʀaui
tuscisquaeʀroce debantde
labiismeisetinconspectu
15 TUOSUNTOMNIA. N ✳ ✳ ✳

(*fol.* 1 v)

Cod. S.
Gall 91
p. 26

p. 31

1 'dmc' sine linea superiori: habet Tisch.   8 'hii.' sic, cum puncto ad finem lineae; *om.* punctum Tisch.   14 'et': *om.* Tisch.   15 post *omnia.* pars litterae 'n' adhuc uisibilis est.

Cod. S.
Gall 912
p. 304

lexbibendicalicembiberunt
ettudummundatauideris
nonmundaberis·perme
enimiurauidicitdms·quia
5 nemopertransietetinos
probrioetinmaledictione
erisinpartetua·etomnes
ciuitatestuaeeruntdeser

p. 309

taeinaeternum·auditu
10 audiuiadmoetnuntios
adcentesmisitdicenscon
crecateuosetueniteaduer
sumeamexsurciteinsuc
nam·purillumdediteinter
15 centesdicnaecontemptū

(*fol.* 2 r)

---

5 'et': *om.* Tisch.   14 *pupillum* Tisch., sed littera 'p' 2° non satis
liquet.   15 lineola super 'u' in *contemptū* non satis liquet, et *om.* Tisch.
Debebat esse *digne-contemptum* (εὐκαταφρόνητον).

INTERhomineSLUSUSTU—S

Cod. S.
Gall 912
p. 303

AdquiSiuiThocTiBiSTulTi

TiamcordiSTuihABiTAuiT

INCAueRNISJeTRARum

5 CONJRehenditmuNiTiO

NemcollisexcelSieTquiA

exAlTASTiSicuTAquilANidu

TuumindedeTRAhamTe

eRiTq·idumeASiNeueSTi p. 310

10 CIO·omNISquiTRANSieT

JeReAmSiBilABiTSicuTSuB

ueRSAeSTSodomAeTCOmoR

RAeTuiciNAeeiuSciuiTATeS

SicSuBueRTAmTediciTdmS

15 OmNIJOTeNS·NONSedeBiT

(fol. 2 v)

1 'tu~s' sic: cf. 'ill~m' Mt xiv 3 c   7 'nidu' apographum meum, fortasse per errorem: nidū Tisch.   12, 14, 15 litterae 'r', 's', et 't' ad fin. abscissae sunt.   Quae suppleui ad initia et fines linearum abscissarum in notis criticis defenduntur.

Comparison of the Fragments with other texts of the LXX.

The verses contained in the S. Gallen fragments are extant in
no other Old Latin MS. Under these circumstances it seemed best
to compare them with the Cambridge text of B, and to bring
together such Latin parallels as were to be found, together with
those variations of Greek MSS from Holmes and Parsons which
might find an echo in a Latin text. It was necessary to give
readings of certain secondary Greek MSS, even where they differed
both from the S. Gallen Palimpsest and from BℵA etc., that the
importance of their occasional points of contact with the Palimpsest
might not be overrated. This is the case for example with
Parsons' 106.

LXX (B)	Fragm. S. Gall.
xvii ^{10}....τοῦ δοῦναι	
ἑκάστῳ κατὰ τὰς ὁδοὺς αὐτοῦ	*Cuique secundum uias eius*
καὶ κατὰ τοὺς καρποὺς τῶν	*et secundum fructum co-*
ἐπιτηδευμάτων αὐτοῦ.	*gitationum eorum red-*
^{11}ἐφώνησεν πέρδιξ,	*dere eis ·* ^{11}*clamauit perdix*
συνήγαγεν ἃ οὐκ	*congregauit quos non pe-*
ἔτεκεν·	*perit ·* multos pariat sibi
ποιῶν πλοῦτον	*filios* adquirens diuitias
αὐτοῦ οὐ μετὰ κρίσεως, ἐν	*suas* non cum iudicio in
ἡμίσει ἡμερῶν αὐτοῦ ἐγκατα-	*dimidio dierum eius dere-*
λείψουσιν αὐτόν, καὶ ἐπ' ἐσ-	*linquent* eum et usq. in no-
χάτων αὐτοῦ ἔσται ἄφρων.	*uissimo suo erit stultus.*
^{12}θρόνος δόξης	^{12}*thronus autem uirtutis.*

Selected Greek variants from the Camb. LXX and Holmes and Parsons. The
symbol ⋏ is used to denote the MSS 22·36·48·51·96·229·231 or a majority of them.
10 αυτου 2°] B^{ath}ℵAQ *Ed. Rom (et MSS c sil);* αυτων B* 106 144 *Compl Ald*
11 συνηγαγεν] pr και ⋏   πλουτον αυτω 144   καταλειψουσιν ⋏ 62   και επ
εσχατων] και επεσχατου 41·49·87·90·91·228; om και 62

From Sabatier [add *m* 355 for *ver.* 10]

10 cogitationum] studiorum *m Aug Vig*   eorum reddere eis] eius *m Aug Vig*
11 congregauit] pr. et *Amb*^{1}/$_2$; collegit *Philastr*   quos] quae *Aug Amb*^{2}/$_2$ *Philastr*
parturiit *Philastr*   multos pariat sibi filios] *no other authority*   adquirens]
faciens *Aug Philastr*   diu. suas] sibi diuitias *Philastr*   indicio] sapientia
Philastr   dimidio] medio *Philastr*   nouissimo suo] nouissimis suis *Aug*^{2}/$_2$;
postremo *Philastr*   stultus] insipiens *Aug*^{2}/$_2$ *Philastr*   12 *init.*] thronus
uirtutis (*om.* autem) *Amb*; sedes autem gloriae *Aug*

LXX (B)

Fragm. S. Gall.

xvii ὑψωμένος

¹³ἁγίασμα ἡμῶν· ὑπομονὴ
Ἰσραήλ,

Κύριε, πάντες οἱ καταλιπόντες
σε καταισχυνθήτωσαν,
ἀφεστηκότες ἐπὶ τῆς γῆς
γραφήτωσαν,
ὅτι ἐγκατέλιπον πηγὴν
ζωῆς τὸν κύριον. ¹⁴ἴασαί με, Κύριε,
καὶ ἰαθήσομαι· σῶσόν με
καὶ σωθήσομαι, ὅτι καύχημά
μου σὺ εἶ. ¹⁵ἰδοὺ αὐτοὶ λέγουσι
πρὸς μέ Ποῦ ἐστιν ὁ λόγος Κυρίου;
ἐλθάτω. ¹⁶ἐγὼ δὲ οὐκ ἐκοπίασα
κατακολουθῶν ὀπίσω σου, καὶ ἡμέραν

exaltatus est. etenim sanc-
tificatio nostra ¹³patientia
illius (?) Istrael.

Dm̄o omnes qui te derelinquerunt confunduntur
qui discesserunt a terra
scribantur in libro mortis
quia derelinquerunt fon-
tem uitae dm̄i. ¹⁴cura me dm̄e
et saluus ero. tu es enim(?)cla-
ritas mea. ¹⁵ecce hii. dicunt
mihi ubi est uerbum dm̄i
ueni ¹⁶ego autem non laboraui subsequens te et diē

Selected Greek variants. 12 υψωμενος] om 144; +απ αρχης τοπος 106; +εξ
αρχης τοπος ג (Qᵐˢ 87 sub ✳) 13 αγιασματος ג υπομονης א* καταισχ.]
πτοηθιησαν ουτοι και μη πτοηθιην εγνω (corr εγω) εσχυνθητωσαν א* καταισχυν-
θητωσαν.....γραφητωσαν] καταισχυνθησονται.....γραφησονται (with varr) ג 22 62 198
επι] απο אᶜᵃ ג 26 62 198 εγγραφητωσαν אᶜⁿ πηγης]+υδατος 62 87 (sub ✳)
14 σωσον....σωθησομαι] om A*ᵛⁱᵈ συ ει] ει συ 41·91·228 26 106 198 οτι] om A
συ] om A 15 ελθατω]+δη ג 41 62 87 (sub ✳); om ελθ. 49·90

From Sabatier [add m 355 for ver. 10]

12 est] Aug Amb (against Gk mss) illius (?)] om. Aug

From Sabatier [add m 698 for ver. 13. The text of Contr. Fulg. Donatistam is
quoted from B.M. Addl. 16896, saec. xi]

13 omnes qui derelinqunt te confundantur, recedentes a te scribantur in libro
mortis, quoniam derelinquerunt te, confundantur recedentes a te fonte uitae. Fulg
ms (derelinquunt...confundentur...scribentur...derelinquerunt te fontem uitae Edd)
uniuersi qui der. te confundantur, recedentes super terram scribantur Aug. c.
adv. Leg
Domine, uniuersi qui te der. terreantur; conf. qui recesser. in terram. Euertentur quoniam derelinquerunt fontem uitae Dominum Aug. Faust. xiii
Domine, omnes qui te derelinquunt confundantur, discedentes a terra euertantur,
qui derelinquerunt fontem uitae Dominum m 698
14 sana me Domine et sanabor, saluum me fac et saluus ero Aug Faust Amb¹/₃
(salua me Amb²/₃ and De xlii Mans) quoniam gloriatio mea tu es Aug quia
gloria mea tu es Amb 15 ubi est uerbum Domini, ueniat Amb²/₃ 16 non
laboraui sequens post te Aug Amb²/₃ et diem hominis non concupiui Aug Hil

LXX (B)

xvii ἀνθρώπου οὐκ ἐπεθύμησα,
σὺ ἐπίστη· τὰ ἐκπορευόμενα διὰ
τῶν χειλέων μου πρὸ προσώπου
σού ἐστιν. ¹⁷μὴ γενηθῇς......

hominis non desideraui
tu scis quae procedebant de
labiis meis et in conspectu
tuo sunt omnia . ¹⁷n......

xxix   Οἷς οὐκ ἦν

¹³νόμος πιεῖν τὸ ποτήριον, ἔπιον·
καὶ σὺ ἀθῳωμένη
οὐ μὴ ἀθῳωθῇς, ¹⁴ὅτι κατ' ἐ-
μαυτοῦ ὤμοσα, λέγει Κύριος, ὅτι
εἰς ἄβατον καὶ εἰς ὀνει-
δισμὸν καὶ εἰς κατάρασιν
ἔσῃ ἐν μέσῳ αὐτῆς, καὶ πᾶσαι
αἱ πόλεις αὐτῆς ἔσονται ἔρη-
μοι εἰς αἰῶνα. ¹⁵ἀκοὴν
ἤκουσα παρὰ Κυρίου, καὶ ἀγγέλους
εἰς ἔθνη ἀπέστειλεν
Συνάχθητε καὶ παραγένεσθε εἰς
αὐτήν, ἀνάστητε εἰς πόλε-
μον· ¹⁶μικρὸν ἔδωκά σε ἐν
ἔθνεσιν, εὐκαταφρόνητον

Lex bibendi calicem biberunt
et tu dum mundata uideris
non mundaberis . ¹⁴per me
enim iuraui dicit dm̄s · quia
nemo pertransiet et in op-
probrio et in maledictione
eris in parte tua · et omnes
ciuitates tuae erunt deser-
tae in aeternum . ¹⁵auditu
audiui a dm̄o et nuntios
ad gentes misit dicens con-
gregate uos et uenite aduersum eam exsurgite in pug-
nam . ¹⁶pu(p)illum dedi te inter
gentes dignaecontemptū

ἐν ἀνθρώποις. ἡ παιγνία σου
ἐνεχείρησέν σοι, ¹⁷ἰτα-
μία καρδίας σου κατέλυσεν
τρυμαλιὰς πετρῶν,

Inter homines lusus tuus
adquisiuit hoc tibi ¹⁷stulti-
tiam cordis tui habitauit
in cauernis petrarum

Selected Greek variants.   16 σου 2°] μου A   εστι] εισι 106

13 επιον] πιοντες επιον Qᵐᵏ sub✱ λ 62   αθωωθης]+οτι πιων πιεσαι (with
variations) AQ λ (πινουσα λ)   14 οτι 1°] om A   οτι εις αβ.....εση] οτι εις αφανι-
σμον και εις αβ. και....εση 86 ; οτι εις αφαν. και εις ονειδισμον και εις αβατον και εις
επικαταρασιν εση λ   καταρασιν] καταραν ℵA 41 106 al; επικαταρασιν λ   εν
μεσω αυτης] εν μεσω μερει αυτης (88) Syr-Hex (μερη 88) ; Βοσορ εν μεσω μερους αυτης
λ 62   15 απεστειλεν] απεστειλαν 62 ; εξαπεστειλε 49-90   εις αυτην] επ αυτην
λ ; εν αυτη 62   αναστητε] pr και λ 62   εις πολεμον]+επ αυτην λ 62
16 μικρον] ιδου μικρον AQ 23 λ alᵐᵘˡᵗ ; οτι ιδου μ. 62   ευκαταφρ.] pr και A 49-90 al
ενεχειρησεν σοι] ενεχειρισε σοι ταυτα λ 62   17 ιταμα] ιταμιαν Q ; και η ατιμια λ ;
ηταμια 106   τρυμαλιας] εν τρυμαλιαις λ 62

There are no quotations in Sabatier.

LXX (B)

xxix συνέλαβεν ἰσχὺν
βουνοῦ ὑψηλοῦ· ὅτι
ὕψωσεν ὥσπερ ἀετὸς νοσσιὰν
αὐτοῦ, ἐκεῖθεν καθελῶ σε.
¹⁸καὶ ἔσται ἡ Ἰδουμαία εἰς ἄ-
βατον, πᾶς ὁ παραπορευόμενος
ἐπ᾽ αὐτὴν συριεῖ· ¹⁹ὥσπερ κατε-
στράφη Σόδομα καὶ Γόμορρα
καὶ αἱ πάροικοι αὐτῆς,
εἶπεν Κύριος
Παντοκράτωρ, οὐ μὴ καθίσῃ....

Fragm. S. Gall.

conprehendit munitio-
nem collis excelsi et quia
exaltasti sicut aquila nidum
tuum inde detraham te
¹⁸eritq. idumea sine uesti-
gio · omnis qui transiet
per eam sibilabit ¹⁹sicut sub-
uersa est Sodoma et Gomor-
ra et uicinae eius ciuitates
sic subuertam te dicit dm̅s̅
omnipotens · non sedebit

Selected Greek variants. **17** οτι υψωσεν] οτι εαν υψωσεις A 239 ; οτι εαν υψωσης Q λ 62 86 al^mult; οτι υψωσας 106 al^p αυτου] εαυτου ℵ ; σου A λ 62 88 106 καθελω σε]+φησι κ̅ς̅ λ 62 **18** πας] pr και Q συριει] εκστησεται και συριει επι πασαν την πληγην αυτης Q λ 62 (with variations) **19** παροικοι] παροικιαι 106 καθιση] κατοικησει A

There are no quotations in Sabatier.

List of words and expressions found in g.

adquirere (ποιεῖν)	Hier xvii 11
(ἐγχειρεῖν, or ἐγχειρίζειν)	xxix 17
aeternus—in aet. (εἰς αἰῶνα)	xxix 14
cauerna (τρυμαλία)	xxix 17
claritas (καύχημα = gloria)	xvii 14
cf. Hier xiii 11 h	
cogitatio (ἐπιτήδευμα)	xvii 10
= Hier xxiii 22 Cypr ;	
but meditatio Hier xi 18 Cypr	
adfectatio Hier xxv 5 Cypr	
studium Hier xvii 10 m Aug	
congregare (συνάγειν)	xvii 11
congregare se (συνάγεσθαι)	xxix 15
curare (ἰᾶσθαι)	xvii 14
derelinquere (καταλείπειν, ἐγκαταλείπειν)	xvii 11, 13
desiderare (ἐπιθυμεῖν)	xvii 16
detrahere (καθαιρεῖν)	xxix 17

digne (= εὐ *in compos.*)
    dignecontemptus (εὐκαταφρόνητος)   xxix 16
discessere (ἀφίστασθαι)   xvii 13
dum (= *Gk. part*)
    dum mundata uideris (ἀθῳωμένη)   xxix 13
enim (ὅτι)   (xvii 14) xxix 14 [*see* quia]
excelsus (ὑψηλός)   xxix 17
exsurgere (ἀνίστασθαι)   xxix 15
habitare in (καταλύειν)   xxix 17
lusus (παιγνία)   xxix 17
maledictio (κατάρασις)   xxix 14
mundari (ἀθῳοῦσθαι)   xxix 13
mundatus uideri (*id*)   xxix 13
munitio (ἰσχύς)   xxix 17
nemo—nemo pertransiet (εἰς ἄβατον)   xxix 14 [*see* sine]
nuntius (ἄγγελος)   xxix 15
opprobrium (ὀνειδισμόν)   xxix 14
pugna (πόλεμος)   xxix 15
pupillus, *or* pusillus (μικρος)   xxix 16
-que (καί)   xxix 18
quia (ὅτι)   xxix 14, 17 [*see* enim]
saluum esse (σώζεσθαι)   xvii 14
sine (= ἀ *priv.*)
    sine uestigio (ἄβατος)   xxix 18 [*see* nemo]
stultitia (ἰταμία)   xxix 17
stultus (ἄφρων)   xvii 11
subsequi (κατακολουθεῖν ὀπίσω)   xvii 16
thronus (θρόνος)   xvii 12
uerbum (λόγος)   xvii 15
uirtus (δόξα)   xvii 12

Points of special interest.

The most striking feature of the S. Gallen fragments (*g*) is the number of interpolations not found in any Greek MS. They are as follows:

Hier xvii 10 eorum] + red*d*ere eis.
      11 peperit] + multos pariat sibi *filios*
      12 thronus] + autem   (= *Aug*)
         exaltatus] + est   (= *Aug Amb*)

Hier xvii 12 sanctificatio] *pr.* etenim

      13 scribantur] + in libro *mortis* (= *contr. Fulg. Don*)

      16 labiis meis] + et ⎫
          sunt] + omnia ⎭

  xxix 15 misit] + dicens

      16 adquisiuit] + hoc (*but cf. the addition of* ταῦτα *in* λ *etc*)

      17 excelsi] + et

      19 uicinae eius] + ciuitates, sic subuertam te

Of a similar nature is the strange rendering of εἰς ἄβατον by *nemo pertransiet* in xxix 14.

There are no Latin quotations for Hier xxix, and not many for the verses of xvii found in *g*. It is tantalizing that the Würzburg Palimpsest (*h*) leaves off just where *g* begins[1], and that a long quotation in Tyconius begins a verse after *g* leaves off.

On the other hand there is a compensation in the quotation of Hier xvii 13 by the Donatist in the '*contra Fulgentium Donatistam*'. This interesting little work (*Migne* xliii 763), ascribed in the MSS to S. Augustine, mainly consists of a Dialogue between a Catholic and a Donatist. The Catholic quotes predominantly from the Vulgate, *but the Donatist from the Old Latin.* This would seem to shew that the Donatists held longer by the old version, and also suggests that the Dialogue is a real one ; for, had the dispute been altogether a piece of literary fiction, the two disputants would hardly have been introduced as quoting from different versions, unless the one version or the other was to be represented as being more accurate or orthodox. The Catholic does indeed correct his opponent for quoting Joh vii 38 in the form *sicut dicit Isaias,* instead of *sicut dicit Scriptura,* but this variant occurs nowhere else, and seems to be a mere blunder of the Donatist.

To return to our text :—in the course of the dispute the Donatist quotes Hier xvii 13 with the addition of *in libro mortis* to *scribantur,* just as in *g*. Is not this enough to found a working hypothesis—I do not say more—that *g* has a text such as was current among the Donatists of the 4th cent. ?

The question is complicated by the reading of *m* 144 and Aug. *contr. Faust* xiii, which have *a terra euertentur* (*m*), *in terram*

---

[1] *g* and *h* are MSS of quite a different size and shape, so that *g* cannot be a stray leaf of *h*.

euertentur (Aug), which seems to point to a variant in the Greek[1]. If this be really so, and not a mere attempt to make sense by emendation instead of addition, the reading of *g Fulg* would seem to be a later correction.

Another point of interest in *g* (which it shares with such African authorities as *de Pascha Computus*) is its coincidences with B, especially the first hand. In these few verses we have

Hier xvii 10 eorum $y = $ αὐτῶν B* 106 al	*but* αὐτοῦ B^{corr}אAQλ etc
	m Aug
xxix 16 μικρον] $g = $ Bא	*but* pr ἰδού AQλ etc
17 et quia exaltasti $g = $ ὅτι	
ὕψωσας 106	
ὅτι ὕψωσεν Bא copt	*but* ὅτι ἐὰν ὑψ. AQλ etc

In the last passage the softening of the construction found in *g* is evidently quite independent of the later Greek reading found in AQ etc.

On the other hand *g* has one reading not known in Greek except as part of a conflation. In xxix 14 *g* has 'in parte tua' corresponding to ἐν μέρει σου, a variant for ἐν μέσῳ αὐτῆς. Here '88' and Syr-Hex[2] have ἐν μέσῳ μέρει αὐτῆς (μερη 88), and in λ we find ἐν μέσῳ μέρους αὐτῆς.

In the Latin of *g* the strangest word is *dignecontemptum* for εὐκαταφρόνητος. I have not been able to find a parallel. Possibly 'bene' was felt to be unsuitable for a compound in a term of abuse.

If I have restored '[cla]ritas' rightly as an equivalent to καύχημα, it must probably be regarded as a substitute for 'gloria'. Similarly we find several instances, even in Cyprian, of 'sermo' for 'uerbum' as an equivalent of ῥῆμα, e.g. Esai xl 8 (*Test* III 58, *de Hab. Virg* § 6).

---

[1] Hier xvii 13 LXX ΑΠΟΤΗΣΓΗΣΓΡΑΦΗΤΩΣΑΝ

     m (Aug) ΑΠΟΤΗΣΓΗΣΣΤΡΑΦΗΤΩΣΑΝ

[2] ܪܚܝܩܐ ܕܡܨܥܬܐ Syr-Hex.

ADDITIONAL NOTES.

1. *On Micah v 2 in Cod. Weingartensis (w).*

The fragmentary Cod. Weingartensis, perhaps the best surviving Latin MS of the Prophets, has lost about half the breadth of the column at Mic v 2, so that the verse runs

ETTUBE...
DOMU...
TIONI...
TA·NU...
MINI...
UTSIS...
IUDA....

What has to be supplied is quite clear, except in the second and third lines. E. Ranke, the discoverer and editor of the MS, restored the passage thus: Et tu be*thleem* | domus *habita*|tionis *efra*|ta· numquid | mini*ma es* | ut sis *in milibus* | iuda..... Now as the Greek of Mic v 2ᵃ is Καὶ σύ, Βηθλέεμ οἶκος Ἐφράθα, [μὴ] ὀλιγοστὸς εἶ τοῦ εἶναι ἐν χιλιάσιν Ἰούδα, it is evident that a gloss of some sort has been inserted in the Weingarten MS after 'domus', of which the letters '-tioni-' are a survival and for which Ranke has conjectured '*habitationis*'. This however has no support, and it is rather too long. I venture to substitute for it '*refectionis*'.

In the Onomastica published by Lagarde no Latin explanation of Bethlehem happens to be given, but I have found in an '*Interpretationes bibliothece*' at the end of a 15th cent. Vulgate in my possession the following line

Bethleem dom' panis 7 dom' refectõis·

'Domus refectionis' was therefore a recognised gloss for Bethlehem, and the occurrence of this name in the text of the Bible, *followed immediately by the word* 'domus', seems to have led to the insertion of 'refectionis' in the text of the Weingarten MS. By substituting 'refec[tioni]s' for the missing letters the required space is exactly filled up, and the presence of the interpolation accounted for.

2.   On the Interpolation in Mc xvi 4 in Cod. Bobiensis.

The interpolation in *k* which describes the Light at the Resurrection runs as follows : su|bito . autem ad horam tertiam | tenebrae diei factae sunt per | totum orbem terrae et des|cenderunt de caelis angeli ‖ et surgent in claritate uiui d̄ī | simul ascenderunt cum eo | et continuo lux facta est|.

The text is evidently not quite sound here.   (1) It is usual to read 'dici tenebrae' for 'tenebrae diei'.   But transpositions are not common in *k*, while confusions of case and the addition and dropping of letters are extremely common.   It is therefore better to simply read with Dr Hort 'die' for 'dici', and to refer to Amos viii 9 ($\sigma\nu\sigma\kappa\sigma\tau\acute{a}\sigma\epsilon\iota \ \epsilon\pi\grave{\iota} \ \tau\hat{\eta}s$ $\gamma\hat{\eta}s \ \epsilon\nu \ \eta\mu\acute{\epsilon}\rho\alpha \ \tau\grave{o} \ \phi\hat{\omega}s$), a passage so often quoted by the Fathers with reference to the Passion that its influence may be legitimately traced in the wording of a story of the Resurrection.

(2) 'Surgent' is evidently wrong.   The accepted conjecture here appears to be 'surgentes' (Hort, Sanday).   But this is open to the objection that in that case the only indication of our Lord's immediate Ascension to Heaven from the tomb, which is evidently implied, would have to be gathered from the words 'cum eo'.   Moreover, as Prof. Robinson has pointed out to me, 'surgere' is inappropriate to the angels.   They *ascended* with our Lord, but He alone *rose* from the dead.   It seems to me that 'surgent' must refer to Christ; I therefore conjecture 'surgente', i.e. 'as He arose'.

For the rather peculiar construction thereby implied—a participle agreeing with something to follow, instead of an abl. abs.—we may compare

Mt viii 1 *k* : et descendentem de montem secuti sunt eum populi multi (= $\kappa\alpha\tau\alpha\beta\acute{a}\nu\tau\sigma s \ \delta\grave{\epsilon} \ \alpha\grave{\upsilon}\tau\sigma\hat{\upsilon} \ \grave{\alpha}\pi\grave{o} \ \tau\sigma\hat{\upsilon} \ \check{o}\rho\sigma\upsilon s \ \mathring{\eta}\kappa\sigma\lambda\sigma\acute{\upsilon}\theta\eta\sigma\alpha\nu \ \alpha\grave{\upsilon}\tau\hat{\omega} \ \check{o}\chi\lambda\sigma\iota \ \pi\sigma\lambda\lambda\sigma\acute{\iota}$).

Here then

surgente......simul ascenderunt cum eo

seems to stand for

$\dot{\epsilon}\gamma\epsilon\rho\theta\acute{\epsilon}\nu\tau\sigma s \ \alpha\grave{\upsilon}\tau\sigma\hat{\upsilon}......\sigma\upsilon\nu\alpha\nu\acute{\epsilon}\beta\eta\sigma\alpha\nu \ \alpha\grave{\upsilon}\tau\hat{\omega}$,

a sentence exactly similar in construction to Mt viii 1.   For the rendering of *simul ascendere cum*, see Mark xv 41 *k*.

INDEX OF PATRISTIC WORKS

QUOTED OR REFERRED TO.

CAMBRIDGE: PRINTED BY J. AND C. F. CLAY, AT THE UNIVERSITY PRESS.